Amber Alert

Amber Alert

(Lord of Wrath)

SEQUELS

JOSEPH DAEGES

Copyright © 2024 Joseph Daeges.

All rights reserved. No part of this book may be reproduced, stored, or transmitted by any means—whether auditory, graphic, mechanical, or electronic—without written permission of both publisher and author, except in the case of brief excerpts used in critical articles and reviews. Unauthorized reproduction of any part of this work is illegal and is punishable by law.

ISBN: 979-8-89419-040-2 (sc)
ISBN: 979-8-89419-041-9 (hc)
ISBN: 979-8-89419-042-6 (e)

Because of the dynamic nature of the Internet, any web addresses or links contained in this book may have changed since publication and may no longer be valid. The views expressed in this work are solely those of the author and do not necessarily reflect the views of the publisher, and the publisher hereby disclaims any responsibility for them.

One Galleria Blvd., Suite 1900, Metairie, LA 70001
(504) 702-6708

Book One

Amber Alert
Lord of Wrath

Dark Skeleton of a Mansion

CHAPTER 1

The Deserted Mansion

One fine summer afternoon, a family of six children relocated from the big city to the wild country. As always with a move to a new lifestyle, there were many things to consider in the beginning, especially for the younger children. Early mornings and late bedtimes were things they had not experienced in a long time.

As the family settled in, their days were full of activities. The children took every minute to explore the new area and all it had to offer. Still, the turbulence and stress of the move were clearly taking their toll upon everyone. Paul, the father, is preoccupied with finances; he is still trying to figure out the terms of the mortgage and what the family could afford to pay. His family is buying a rather strange home—it is a mansion, but it is a little run-down and needed some mending here and there. The structure of the house is solid, but the inside is old and battered.

Obviously in their excitement, Paul and his family had overlooked these details; they were just pleased about the cost and general quality of the house. And the timing could not have been more perfect; everything is happening briefly. Each minute that went by got them a little closer to the moment when they could finally be settled in the home, they can call their own, enjoying the little routines of life.

For Paul and Eva especially, this is the culmination of a lifelong dream and a lifetime of sacrifice and saving. On the morning of their move into their new home, they made the rounds of their five-bed room apartment for the last time, turning in their keys on their way to the mansion. This new home is their dream in reality; exactly what the family needs.

Paul's character is a perfect mix; independent and persistent. Paul had encountered many difficulties in life, and he always came out on top. Eva, Paul's wife, is a calm person who did not like disturbance. She is to some extent unenthusiastic to changes. Angelo, Paul, and Eva's oldest son are more bashful than his parents and hates to be fooled. He is a clever child, always one step ahead. He is a smart little man, but as for his brothers, Alex Patrick, and Ron, they were more responsive and efficient with a fondness for adventure.

Angelo's two sisters, Cecilia, and Angelica shared similar calm temperaments. A person who did not know them would assume that they were twins because they would rather keep their exclusive company together unceasingly. They seemingly adore their brothers, but still liked to be left alone doing their own little things. The sibling's ages ranged from six to eleven years. Eva thought she needs a massive source of energy to cope with their poles apart demands.

Paul is busy checking what needs to be repaired. There were six bedrooms on the second floor, and a living room, dining room, kitchen, and playroom on the first floor. He just checked the windows and looked outside. The house sat on ten acres' plain, so there is plenty of space for the children to play and have fun.

Just twenty meters west of the mansion is struggling lake with clean meager water coming from the mountains less than a mile away, Paul thought he saw someone in there when they had arrived but shrugged the idea thinking he must be so tired to imagined things. Many trees were gracefully outstretched downhill and some ridges creasing the vast plains. There is a plant bed with tools and unopened seed packs that were left unfinished near the creek. The previous owner might have attempted planting a few crops, Paul wondered what happened to that.

The nearest neighbor is about one mile away—perfect, Paul thought, because it gave the place a unique sense of privacy. The mansion had its own well and is situated near a lake where the children could go fishing and camping in the summertime. Paul would not have to worry about their campfires spreading to the trees, because the lake had a natural sandy beach about 150 feet deep.

One thing about the mansion had caught Paul's attention: all the personal belongings the prior resident had left there for no apparent reason. Just another bank repo, he thought—never stopping to consider that there might be a far more foreboding reason.

The first weeks were busy: they moved and unpacked bag after bag and box after box. They knew they would be living with a mess for a good couple of months.

While Paul is wandering in the property trying to inspect everything that needs repair, his wife Eva is occupied with cleaning out old food that had been left in the fridge and cupboards. Some seemed to have been there for a long time, as evidenced by a great deal of mold. So, mustering all her courage, Eva tackled the chore, carefully and diligently throwing away all the leftover food and personal belongings. In the course of her work, she discovered a little door in the kitchen wall on the right side of the stove. Her curiosity is piqued, but she decided to wait until the next day to explore it. She reasoned that it would be difficult to explore, as she had piled almost all the trash in the hallway and still could barely walk through the kitchen.

While Eva worked in the kitchen, the children began arguing over who would have this room or that one. Then a fight broke out. Eva had to run upstairs to restore order among the children. Meanwhile, Paul is exploring the outbuildings to see what they had to offer.

A loud, happy "Yes!" rang out from the barn, and for a moment, the children forgot all about fighting and ran to find out why Daddy is so happy. Upon their arrival, they saw their father looking over some old cars, a pickup truck parked behind the building, and a large tractor loader.

"This is worth money," Paul said. "I have hit the jackpot—I have worked hard all of my life, so I just knew someday I'd be lucky! Here I am today, in a barn where luck has finally opened her arm to me." He tried to start the tractor, but it is out of fuel. "Well, I will try the pickup," he said, "Maybe it will run, at least." He checked the truck's fuel level, discovered that it is half-full, and took a chance. It started and soon is running smoothly. "My goodness!" he exclaimed again joyfully.

He opened the door of the barn to clear the smoke out while he warmed up the truck's motor. Please, Paul checked the brake fluid, which is good, and then he examined the brakes, which looked new. With much anticipation, he got behind the steering wheel and engaged the transmission into reverse; nothing happened. Hmmm, Paul thought, maybe it is missing transmission fluid. How long has this pickup been sitting in the barn, anyway?

He stepped out of the pickup, opened the hood for the second time, and pulled out the dipstick for the transmission fluid. It is dry. "Well, here's the problem," he said aloud, "and not a big one, I hope." He sat down in his car, drove down to the village, bought two quarts of transmission fluid, and then returned to the mansion.

By then, food is ready to be served and Eva had rung the dinner bell. Settling into chairs all around the table, the family gathered for the first time since they had moved into the mansion. Sure enough, they had stories to exchange.

Eva could not stop talking about how horrible the kitchen is and a load of garbage that she had had removed from it. Paul countered by complaining that the food is too salty.

Eva insulted, replied, "Well, you know, mister, you never did complain before, and I expect you not to start this game now." Even the children started to complain about the salt in their food. Eva is frustrated. First, she had had to clean up the huge mess in the kitchen, and now she had to deal with the whole family being unhappy. Eva gave the children a look and warned them to stay out of the kitchen. "There's only one chef in the family," she said. She would not allow anyone to tamper with her cooking.

At this point, Paul took the hint and invited his wife to sit down at the table and enjoy the delicious meal that she had presented to them. Still simmering, Eva came in from the kitchen and sat down with the rest of the family; at least they could not say she is not at the table with them. Alex, one of the boys, made his point by filling his mother's bowl and presenting it to her, saying, "Here Mom, chef of the twenty-first century." Eva turned red as an apple, and the rest of the family had a good laugh. She is sensitive about the whole thing because it is the first time that she had ever heard any complaints about her food. Eva is a master chef; her skill in the kitchen is well-known in the area, and she had cooked for several wealthy people and even government agencies.

Eva wanted to prove herself right away, without a minute's hesitation she picked up a spoon and took a bite of food. Almost immediately she spits it out—and then it is a free-for-all, with everyone saying, "You see? You cannot even eat it yourself! What did you do?"

Eva is mortified, sitting speechless in her chair – it cannot be. But she soon collected herself and replied, "One of you kids think you are funny, I better not see you kids fooling around the kitchen. If I ever catch any one of you in here—well, you will see. I will fix the problem. You have my word on that."

The children looked upset and left the table hungry, quietly deciding to go get some cake. While the children were looking for their dessert, Paul had a little chat with his wife. "My dear, what's the matter with you?"

"I don't know," she replied, "but I have never had any problems cooking before."

Just then, they heard an excited shout from one of the older boys, "Oh! Come, hurry Dad!" Paul stood up and hurried to the window to see what the problem is.

It is the pickup with the transmission problem, rolling out of the barn. "I probably forgot to put the transmission into park," Paul said. Eva saw her chance. "Now what's the matter with you?" she asked silly.

Paul said nothing, simply turning red, and walked to the barn. He arrived just in time to stop the pickup from running into another small outbuilding next to the barn. He noticed that there is a blackbird lying on the barn floor where the pickup had been. This is like a scene from one of those horror movies, he thought, and he kicked the bird out of the barn. To his surprise, it suddenly roused itself and took off, flying high into the sky as if to laugh at the poor, confused human. The bird soon disappeared into the blue sky, and Paul thought nothing more about it.

Paul went back to business settling into the pickup and engaged the transmission into drive. This time he can drive a few feet; he noticed some smoke coming out from under the hood. That is not bad, he thought at first. He turned the motor off to check the problem and saw that the transmission fluid is overflowing. Now Paul is really confused, he did not want to say anything to Eva because he knew she is not in a good mood. After tinkering a bit, he finally had the pickup fixed and ready to go. He left the barn feeling a little bit better about the whole situation. That is one thing I accomplished today. At least something is going our way, finally. He is hoping things would turn around for Eva also.

In the mansion, Eva is determined to find what happened with her cooking and solve it once and for all. She is walking around the kitchen from one end to the other, all her senses alert, trying to figure out what sort of prank had been pulled. She had never had that problem before, but you never knew—the children were getting older, and maybe they were ready to do anything to get a little attention and have some fun.

After a while, Eva realized that she is wasting her time, so she decided to continue to the rest of her tasks. As she went to replace the garbage bag, she saw an enormous rat just behind the trash can. Eva almost fainted. For a moment she stood paralyzed; unable to move or say anything. Boy, that is a big one, she thought. She had never seen such a thing in her entire life. But the rat is as scared as she was. Quick as lightning, it disappeared without a trace.

At this point, Eva is just waiting for Paul to get home so she could unload her frustration and anger, but she kept working. Added to her frustration is the realization that the day is almost over and not one thing they needed for bed is unpacked. The too-salty dinner is still sitting on the dining room table. Exhausted, Eva sat down for a while and took a well-deserved five, but her mind is preoccupied with all the other tasks to be done before night came.

Remembering that none of the beds were up, she told her son Angelo to see what Dad is doing and urged him to come back to the house to install the bed if he did not want to sleep on the floor.

Angelo is on his way to the barn when the blackbird swooped down to peck his head. This really topped off a stressful day for Angelo. He threw a rock at the bird screaming, "Get away from me!" Wiping the fresh blackbird droppings out of his hair, he stormed into the barn and said, "That dirty bird shouldn't peck people's heads."

Paul had a good laugh and replied, "Well, son, this is how we get smart."

Then he paused a moment before asking, "What color is the bird?" "It's black," Angelo responded.

At this, Paul became a little nervous and annoyed, but he did not comment further. "Do you need anything?" he asked Angelo.

"Mom asked me to tell you to hurry back to the house and put the bed together if you want to sleep on a bed tonight," Angelo said.

"Oh yeah," Paul said. "The day's almost over, I will be right their son."

As Paul and Angelo walked back to the house together, the bird came back, and this time it swooped down again to peck on both of their heads. "You scumbag!" Paul exclaimed, "You should be happy now and not peck the head of the one who freed you from that pitch black barn!"

"Dad, it's only a bird," Angelo said, "What will Mom say when she sees us?" Unsure of what they would face when they walked into the house, Paul quietly wiped the bird droppings from Angelo's head and then from his own. They entered the house to find Eva still in a daze from seeing the big rat in the kitchen.

"What is the matter, dear? You look like you just saw a ghost. Your hair is standing straight up." "Very funny!" Eva replied. "No,—I was just making a statement. In all the years I have known you, I have never seen you like this."

Reassured, Eva said, "I just saw the biggest rat I have ever seen in my life behind the trash can. What a nightmare! It has been one thing after another, nonstop Paul. I said it will be remarkably interesting to live here, dear." Eva wrote a note to remind Paul that when he drove to the store to buy the biggest rat trap he could find; first thing in the morning. Then she said, "We don't have much time left to put up the beds for the night."

Paul immediately began looking for all the parts of the beds so he could put them together while Eva is busy sweeping all the rooms.

The couple's teamwork had been their best weapon, they trust each other, and they focus on each other's strength gaining control over a demanding situation like this.

It had been a bit scary at times, but the beauty of the mansion, with its unique charm and character, compensate the difficulties they encountered during the day. Night came, everybody is getting ready to hit the sack. The siblings were busy finding their respective spots and started dozing off.

Within a couple of hours, a problem started. A loud laugh and a scary noise came from the direction of the girls' room. The girls saw two bright, shining eyes looking at them. Terrified they screamed and covered their faces with their pillows. Paul leaped out of bed and running to see what the problem was when he stepped on the tail of the big rat from the kitchen. He stood there, frozen like a statue, and watched the rat run straight into the nearest room—his bedroom.

With their father's encouragement, the girls eventually calmed down and fell asleep, Paul returned to his room. Just as he stepped into bed, he spotted the same scary face that the girls had seen earlier. Damn that rat! Paul did not want to wake up his wife; he had had enough trouble for one day and could not deal with any more problems. If Eva is sleeping, everything will be okay, Paul thought. How long could this monster stay in the room without him going crazy? He thought for sure it was the devil or some evil spirit that had come to destroy his peaceful night. Finally, the rat decided that it had enough and continued its way. Paul realized that this was the rat that Eva had seen in the kitchen, so he leaped out of the bed again to quietly close the bedroom door behind him. Then he went back to bed to finally have a moment of peace and relaxation.

Not long after Paul fell asleep, Eva woke up with a start; someone is walking on the floor above her head. She decided to wake Paul. "What is your problem now?" Paul asked, a little cranky. "Paul, someone or something is walking in the room above my head—it's scaring me."

At this point, Paul went to the storage room and found some earplugs and passed them to his wife. Eva is not too happy, but she agreed to put them on, and in less than ten minutes she is sleeping like an angel.

Morning came too soon, and all siblings had the same question at the breakfast table, "Did you see anything different yesterday?" Perhaps they meant the humongous rat sprightly wandering at night.

To this Angelo replied, "Well, I know one thing. If I ever come across that blackbird, well, he'd better fly high because I won't miss him." At that, all his siblings started laughing at Angelo's obvious frustration and humiliation. Then the conversation turned to the menu for the day with Eva commenting no one is going to play a trick on her again.

At breakfast, everything went well; everyone seemed happier and calmed down from the stressful transfer a day before. Soon they all seemed to have forgotten about the previous day's misfortunes. They were banking on the hope that it is just an isolated event and there would be no more disturbances that would take place.

After breakfast, Paul drove to the store to find a good solution for the monstrous rat that had terrorized his family most of the night. Paul looked at the items on the pest-control aisle but could not really find anything that fit the description of the beast. The cashier is quite amused by Paul's "apparent" fertile imagination. Paul finally decided to get supplies for any emergency that might occur, taking precautions against the unknown. At least I will be prepared for whatever happens, he thought.

As he is coasting up the driveway toward the mansion, he noticed some fresh tire tracks near the mailbox; the postman must have come. He felt an irrational wave of fear and chastised himself, that eerie feeling that something bad is going to happen. But when he opened the mailbox, a horrible smell wafted out of it. He could not bear the smell. The stench is like the bird droppings from the previous day. Paul gathered his courage and grabbed the mail out of the box. Again, he had that funny feeling but brushed the idea off. "Preposterous! What bad could happen? Oh no, I am getting paranoid."

He drove back to the mansion and slowly stepped out of the car and walked to the house. Eva is more than happy to see him back. She is glad he had found a rat trap but said she is afraid that it would not be big enough.

"Well, I looked through the entire store, and this is the biggest that I could find for the size of the rat we have in this house," Paul said. "The store owner is amused at my dilemma when I told them about the monstrous rat, they all thought I was hallucinating." Then Paul and Eva started planning the day, organizing everything and the logistics of the move, because they did not have much vacation time to spend. Paul agreed to focus on the most important thing first and leave everything else alone for the time being. So, while the rest of the family focused on installing the furniture and moving into the house, Paul had hoped to have the machinery in the barn working. However, he decided to put it on the side so he could concentrate on finishing the move into the mansion. He would not enter the barn until everything is up and running again.

Eva decided to wash a load of clothes, so she went to the laundry room and had everything ready to go. The washing machine looked new; Eva opened the lid loaded in the clothes added the detergent and closed the lid. The washing machine seems to work fine and when the cycle is done, she went back to the laundry room and found, to her surprise, the clothes were dirtier than when she put them in. Horrified, she called her husband, who found out that the coil in the hot water tank is rusty. Paul turned off the waterline, disconnected everything, and drained the tank. It turned out that the rusty water is coming from the reserve part of the tank. Paul went back to the store, this time to buy a hot water tank.

After the installation, the water seemed normal, so Paul decided to keep the receipt and call the realtor to report the problem. However, yet another problem is on the horizon. When Paul picked up the phone, the line is dead. He took out his cell phone and talked to the operator, who connected him to the telephone service in the village.

The telephone repairman arrived, and as he went about his duties, he explained to Paul his frustration—this was not the first time this problem had occurred. He told Paul that he believed the mansion is haunted, although he is not sure of it and could not explain why he believed it is.

Already under stress, Paul replied, "I might've bought myself a lemon, and now my whole family will suffer from my stupidity." Paul had a strong character, though. On previous occasions when he had faced a complicated situation, he found that if he is tenacious enough, he would finally conquer it, overcoming obstacles one by one until the entire problem is solved.

Therefore, the proud father never gave up. For a while, everything is fine and peaceful. Everyone seemed fine and had forgotten the disorder when they moved in. Then, one morning during breakfast, the big rat reappeared out of nowhere, terrifying Eva. Everyone was taken by surprise.

Paul soon arrived at Eva's side to comfort her, trying to reassure her that he will do something about that rat. Just then, Angelo raced into the house, screaming that he had been attacked again by the blackbird, and this time he wanted revenge. In a rage, Angelo took a shower and then headed right back outside, and all the other members of the family had a good laugh at his expense. "That bird needs to go," Angelo said from the kitchen doorway, "Why doesn't it do this to anyone else except me?"

Paul replied. 'One thing is for sure; I will deal with this black bird the next time I see it. That is a promise, son".

With such an auspicious start to the day, Paul considered calling an expert in paranormal events to study the phenomena occurring in the mansion. He did not discuss the idea with his family for that fear they would think it is ridiculous, but Paul held on to this thought.

Later that day he spent hours considering it, weighing all the benefits of doing so against the chance that he may be ridiculous. He chuckled, thinking he is being paranoid again. Paul had no way of knowing he is about to have an experience that would result in hours of pain and frustration. He only knew one thing at that point, and that he should stay strong and firm to convince his family that this is a good place to live. It is the perfect home for them—a large house on beautiful land—and Paul figured if he succeeded in solving the strings of the problem starting from day one, his children would soon love the place and Eva will not let him feel that she regrets the transfer.

This was not the first time that Paul found himself in a challenging situation, and as always, he was confident he would be able to fix everything. He is thinking, the issues with this mansion can never bring me down. With conviction, Paul muttered, "Bring it on!"

CHAPTER 2

The suspected Flying saucer

As time went by and the family became adjusted to the rural life. It is amazing how the children did not complain about anything or made comments comparing their life in the city and the mansion. Paul had had a lot on his plates these past few days. He worked during weekdays; he stops by the grocery store to get what they need. At home after work, he fixed the window or the cupboard. During weekends, Paul and the kids finally had the time to play in the garden. Paul would put up the tent for the kids. The children helped Paul getting rid of those gardening tools and seed packs left by the previous owner. Paul thought the kids are loving the place already. Perfect! Everything is simply perfect.

At the breakfast table one morning, Paul suggested.

"I know we certainly have some sort of problem here; I am not done fixing the house yet," he said to Eva, "but I have decided to hold a housewarming party and invite the rest of the family to celebrate with us in our new home. After all, this is a family tradition, and we should respect that."

Paul had not been sure how to broach the subject, but when he walked downstairs and found his wife in the kitchen quietly sipping her coffee, he thought, Okay, it is time to ask Eva—it is now or never.

It had already been three months since they bought and moved into their new home, and if he waited any longer, the housewarming party would never happen. So, he sat down by his wife and had delicately suggested.

Eva set her cup down and glaring at him. "How do you expect me to have a housewarming party if you and the children won't even eat my cooking anymore?"

"Well, we could always buy premade food, like party trays and things like that."

To Paul's surprise, Eva agreed to the idea, and she told Paul that this would be the first item on her to-do list: she would head to the store shortly to buy everything they needed for the big occasion.

Paul is pleased. After giving Eva a huge hug, he went back upstairs to change into work clothes so he could clean up the yard around the house. The children were all still sleeping, he is very discreet and careful not to wake them. He quickly changed clothes and went downstairs to the kitchen. He swallowed the last bite of his doughnut, washed it down with coffee, and then went toward the barn.

He felt a little reluctant to enter the barn, still remembering the bad experiences he had had in there previously. And the bird. That blackbird!

Let us see if the tractor will start this morning since I got five gallons of gas yesterday. For a moment Paul is excited and hopeful. He poured gas into the tractor's tank and turned the key in the ignition. The tractor started right away without giving any problems and it seemed to be running perfectly. That made a good start to the day! Now, Paul would be able to hook the brush hog onto the tractor to mow around the house. He backed the tractor out of the barn and then went back inside to see if he could find any clipper attachments in there. As he is walking around in the barn, he found a couple of things he needed, but something caught his eye—a flash of something appeared over where the tractor had been parked Paul's curiosity is strong. What could it be? Paul thought, in a fit of whimsy. He bent over to pick up the shiny object. It is a key. Probably a key to some door upstairs, he thought. I will put it on a nail just in case I need it later. Not thinking any more about it, Paul hung up the key and rushed back out to install the brush hog onto the tractor.

Back at the house, everyone is ready to start the day. The children had just finished their breakfast and were about to walk out of the house. Angelo is a bit reluctant to step out because of the blackbird, and the rest of his brothers and sisters teased him about it. While the other children were up and running like rabbits, Angelo is still standing in the kitchen, watching them through the window, clearly ill at ease. Paul still in the house, encouraged Angelo to go outside, but nothing he said is working—Angelo just did not want to leave the house. Finally, Paul said, "Well, son, I will let you drive the tractor if you come out. "To this Angelo replied, "Really!? I will be right out." Buoyed by his success, Paul went to get the tractor and drove by the house to pick up his son.

As soon as Angelo stepped outside, the blackbird is there again. Angelo did not see it right away, but Paul did. "Where is this menace coming from?" Paul muttered. "I haven't seen you all morning, and I have been up for at least five hours! What do you want eh birdie?" As soon as Angelo mounted onto the tractor, the motor stalled. "Let's just start this tractor again—not a problem," Paul said.

He turned the key off and then back on. Over and over, Paul tried to start the motor, it is not working. Furious, he told Angelo to stay in the tractor and do not move. He stepped down from the tractor and checked all the battery connections. After that, he climbed back on, grabbed the steering wheel, and tried to crank the motor again. Nothing happened.

By then Angelo needed to go to the restroom, so Paul told him to go. As soon as Angelo stepped off the tractor, it started up—instantly. Paul jumped off the tractor, gave the tire a good kick, and ran into the house. Angelo is still in the restroom. Paul walked up to his bedroom, loaded a pistol, then went back downstairs. He promised his son he will take care of bird next time he sees it. By then Angelo is ready to go, and they walked back outside together.

Paul told Angelo he is waiting for the blackbird; he is going to deal with the problem once and for all. They stood there for a few minutes, waiting, but nothing happened. There is no sign of the blackbird, so Paul told Angelo to hop onto the tractor. Soon the boy is behind the wheel, ready to go. As Paul hopped on behind him, he looked down and saw the bird pecking at the back tire. "My goodness, you scumbag! what do you think you are doing." Paul jumped off the tractor immediately and ran to the back tire, but by then the wise bird is gone. Paul climbed back onto the tractor, furious that the bird seemed to be smarter than he is.

The tractor is still running, however, and Paul is happy about that. He decided to start cutting the grass around the house in hope of getting at least something done before Eva is back from the store. After all, it had been his idea to have a housewarming party the very next Sunday.

Eva finished up her shopping, made a quick stop at the gas station, and went straight home. As she pulled into the driveway, she noticed that Paul is on the tractor and had succeeded in accomplishing some of the tasks necessary to keep their housewarming party on schedule. Eva then began unloading the car and started on putting the groceries away in the kitchen.

Paul is working tirelessly to get the large yard cut when suddenly; the tractor's back tire went flat. Although this is the tire the big blackbird had been pecking, Paul never gave it any serious thought. He told himself that the tire probably had deteriorated from having been in the barn for so long and went flat when it is finally put to work.

Paul removed the tire from the tractor, loaded it onto the pickup, and drove to a service station in town to have it patched. The mechanic said, "It will be ready in an hour. Do you have anything to do in the meantime?"

"Yes, sure," Paul said. "Let me give you my phone number, and I will be on my way." Then he called Eva to ask her to come to pick him up from the service station.

"Not a problem," she said. "I will be there in fifteen minutes—just wait for me outside." Fifteen minutes later, Eva and Paul were on their way back home. Before getting out of the car, Paul leaned over to kiss his wife. "I love you," he said.

"I love you too," she replied, looking bothered by another matter, "but something seems to be extremely wrong here," Eva explained that

Angelo had told her about the blackbird. "Angelo said you saw that bird again, pecking at the tire. He also said you jumped off the tractor, but before you were able to take action, it had already flown off."

"It's just a bird dear, a very persistent annoying blackbird," Paul said. "After all, look at all of the work I have accomplished around the house. It looks a lot better than it did when we first bought it." Eva agreed, and their conversation moved on to other subjects such as how many friends and families were invited to the housewarming party, and how many might come.

Soon, Paul is back in the barn, starting more projects. He had had no time to examine the loader, as he had been faced with so many problems one after another. So, he decided to have a look at the big loader and try to get it moving. If he succeeded, then he could continue working around the barn, the garage, and the house.

After about an hour and a half, Paul's cell phone rang. It is the mechanic calling to report that the tire is not repairable. "Whatever punctured the tire must have been a very sharp object," he said. "It cut through the core inside of the tire."

Paul jumped off the loader. "Are you sure?" he asked nervously. "One hundred percent sure," the mechanic replied. He asked.

Paul if there was someone he did not get along with—an enemy, perhaps. The mechanic went on to add that the cut is well executed is that he rarely saw anything like it, but generally, when did, it was done on purpose. At that point, Paul could not say anything. He tried to put his thoughts in order, preoccupied with the fact that the blackbird had been pecking at the same tire.

"Well, I don't know what to tell you Sir, but I think I have an idea of what happened," the mechanic said. "If I can be of any help in court, you can count on me."

"Thank you," Paul said. "How much would it cost to replace the tire?"

"This will cost you six hundred fifty dollars, without tax." "That's a lot of money, but I guess I don't have a choice," Paul said. "Go ahead and change the tire." Paul hung up the phone. He is rather upset but managed to keep his cool. He went back to the barn and continued to work on his next project: the loader. He methodically ran through his maintenance checklist and was pleased to see that everything looked good. With anticipation, he sat down to try to start the loader. When it started up without any problem, he felt encouraged. He thought, something good must happen to me today—it is not always bad luck after all!

While their parents worked around the house and barn, the children had a good time at the lake fishing. As dinnertime approached, they agreed to call it a day and return home. On the way back, however, something strange grabbed their attention. It is an impression in the grass—a huge circle as if a big round soccer ball had just touched down. Excited, the children ran to the house yelling, "Daddy! Daddy! Daddy, come and see what we have found!"

Rather surprised to see his children so worked up, Paul decided to go and check it out. As he walked closer to the ring, he could understand why the children had been so excited by their discovery.

"Well, kids," he said, "it looks like we had some strange visitors that came and landed on our property." As Paul spoke, he suddenly thought of all the strange things that had been happening around the house; from the events of their first day, up to this discovery. He stood there for a moment without saying anything, and then he said, "Whatever you do, you must stay together and not leave anyone behind. Make sure that when you leave the house together, you count to make sure all of you come back together too."

Angelo is not with them at the time, and neither Paul nor any of the other children thought much about it. Everybody knew he is furious about the bird and reluctant to go anywhere on the property. It would not be the first time that Angelo decided to stay home with his mother.

As Paul walked back to the house with the children, he tried to stay positive but sensed that something had gone terribly wrong. He is just about to find out that his intuition is correct when he arrived home. Angelo is not there. Paul ran upstairs to see if perhaps the boy had hidden in his room. He tried going back to the lake, at the back of the mansion, the barn, no signs of Angelo. Finding nothing, he came back downstairs and in a flash is on his way back to the area recently discovered by his children.

Paul reached the flattened circle, dropped to his knees, and started to cry. Where is Angelo? He stayed there, silent, and heartbroken when suddenly he remembered the blackbird that had assaulted Angelo—the same bird that had assaulted him too. "Oh, my goodness!" he exclaimed. This blackbird might be a sign that something is going to happen to my son, Paul reasoned as other thoughts ran wild through his mind. Where can he possibly go? Aliens.

The fresh evidence of the circle found on the grass behind the barn would convince anyone of touch down of one of their vessels. The circle pointed to a possible reality that Angelo might have been abducted by aliens. Simply, this blackbird could be a spy for an unknown perpetrator, and he could be waiting in the nearby wooded mountain. At this point, Paul is on the verge of a major breakdown, but he did not want to alarm the rest of the family.

The questions were racing through his mind, where is he? Where will I start looking? Who would take my son? The blackbird, does he have something to do with this? The large circle at the back of the barn, what is that? is this all related? Paul could not come up with a clear answer. He is in such distress that it changed his entire personality and attitude.

"I need to find Angelo no matter what! Oh, Eva, this will break her heart." Paul murmured, "How?" Walking back home, his heart broken, his mind spinning trying to make sense of Angelo's disappearance, all Paul could think about is the possibility that his son is lost. He is ready to give up anything, even the mansion that he and Eva had dreamed of—everything—to get Angelo back.

Walking like a man who had just lost everything, Paul arrived home. He is in tears, and the other children realized something is very wrong. They had never seen their dad cry before. Eva spoke first. "Where's my boy?" she asked anxiously. "Do you know where Angelo is? I had the feeling something happened to him. Please do not tell me you do not know where our son Angelo is! I am calling the police…"

Paul could not give her an answer; he is visibly upset and appeared to be on the brink of a nervous breakdown.

The remaining children stood by their parents, frozen by the atmosphere. There were heavy tears running down their faces as they wondered what is going on. Angelo's brother and sisters knew that their brother is the cleverest one in the whole family. They thought that maybe this is a prank. Paul told the rest of the children that he had the feeling that Angelo is not playing any prank on them and someone might have taken him. However, giving a second thought to his children's suggestion, Paul decided to go with the children to see if Angelo is, in fact, playing hide and seek with them. A couple of hours were spent searching for Angelo, nothing, not even a pair of shoes. Paul walked back home with the remaining children and his mind is still running wild.

Stepping into the mansion, he looked at Eva who is frantically crying and reassured her that everything would be alright, and he begged her to give a couple more hours before calling the police. Maybe Angelo would come out of his hidden place. "I will do everything to find our son and bring him back to us," he said.

After a couple of agonizing hours, there is still no sign of Angelo. The more time that flew by, the more Paul realized that abduction is probably the case. Paul paused for a moment, then remembered the blackbird that had swooped down on Angelo's head. Paul then froze for a moment. Suddenly, he looked up at Eva and said, "Maybe a neighbor nearby abducted Angelo, and as a cover-up, burned a circle on the grass to make us believe that an alien really did take our son." Without losing any time, Paul reached for the phone and dialed 911 and asked the police to come and investigate the situation.

A policeman soon arrived at the mansion. When he heard Paul's story, he seemed unsurprised, strange things had already happened there, but no one had been able to solve the mysteries. Standing with the family at the kitchen table, the policeman told the remaining children to stick together and be extra cautious. Then, he demonstrated some self-defense moves just in case they came face-to-face with the perpetrator. Once the children left the kitchen, the policeman, Paul, and Eva sat down at the table. For a moment, no one spoke.

After a couple of minutes, the policeman broke the silence, explaining to the distraught parents that this sort of disappearance was not unique and that it was not the first time he had been called to this address. The officer reassured Paul and Eva and begged them to stay put, saying that maybe if they were patient with the system, they might solve the mystery and get their son back." Paul and Eva simply sat quietly, thinking.

Finally, Paul said, "This is all good to know. How can I be sure this will not happen to another one of my children? I can't just lock them up in the mansion."

The officer then said, "From all the case history associated with this place, it was always a single boy who disappeared. We checked back with previous owners, and they all said the same thing."

Eva felt like she is dying inside. She had litanies of questions, and her mind is spinning faster than she could process. In tears, she said, "Sir, can you tell me how many other families went through the same trauma?"

The officer replied, "Off the top of my head, I'd say at least three families have been victims of this cruel crime. The reason why we have not been able to shed light on these mysteries is that every family packed up and left the mansion without giving anyone any addresses or telephone numbers. The officer said, "We are sure that from time to time these parents come back into the neighborhood with their families to see if any new clues have been found, but they do not announce themselves."

Eva replied, "Can you blame them, Sir? I know you want to put an end to this, but I am sure you realize how hard it is for a mother to lose a child."

The officer answered, "Yes, I do realize how hard this must be for you—to get up in the morning, knowing that your son has vanished. I know how painful staying here could be for you, and I am here to promise you that if you decide to stay, we can solve the problem. You will have all the help you need from the police department. I can guarantee you that the department will do everything in its power to resolve this loss. Also, we will make sure that you have security: we will assign an officer to come every day to patrol the area. On the other hand, if you pack up and leave, you give us truly little to work with. You know, the last family that lived here, about two years ago, just moved away not too long ago. I can tell you that they had the same problem as you are having today."

Paul, visibly unhappy, said, "Then why in the world did the listing agent not mention anything about this situation? If I had read about this, we would still have our son with us."

The officer said, "That I can't tell you. The only thing I can do is work with you, so you are reunited with your son."

Paul and Eva thanked the officer and told him they were willing to work with the police to solve this. "After all," they said, "if we find our son—and maybe not just our son, but other people's sons also—then we'll have a story worth telling."

To this, the officer replied, "You are brave parents. I don't know any other parents as brave as the ones I am talking to today." With that, the officer left to go back to his cruiser. Paul and Eva, still sitting at the table, discussed their next move.

The officer returned to the mansion soon after he had left, having forgotten a small detail about a previous event that occurred in the mansion. Because the event is considered confidential, the officer told Paul and Eva that these details are confidential to avoid panic in the village. Not until they know what really happened to the boy. It targeted an ex-owner's activities, mentioning he is still living around the mansion.

The officer told Paul and Eva to keep a sharp eye on any former owners because they suspected one of them is wanted as a suspect. Then, giving the grieving parents his business card; he left for the police station to report everything to his superior. It is clear to Paul and Eva that the choice of how to proceed lay solely in their hands. They decided to let the situation rest for the remainder of the day.

While the children spent the out by the lake, Paul and Eva discussed what to do next, considering options, will they move out like the other families? Still seated at the kitchen table, they looked at all the angles, the pros, and the cons of staying put. First, money is now becoming a big problem; unexpected expenses of the move itself had exceeded the calculated cost of the budget. Paul and Eva were forced to set their priorities according to the budget. Paul liked the fact that the mansion is within walking distance from work; however, he had a hard time staying put. He could not get over the fact that Angelo, his son, is missing. Only for the love of Angelo is he willing to stay put, in the hope that he would be reunited with his son.

Paul and Eva want their son back no matter what the costs, sacrifices, and efforts were. They decided not to leave Angelo behind. Eva liked that the kitchen is big, with a lot of cupboards to put all the dishes in. On the other hand, she would have to live in constant fear, worrying about her children. They took a quarter and flipped it in the air. Heads, they would stay put. Tails, well, they would have to move. It fell on heads, so they decided to stay put and keep a close eye on the remaining children.

Paul and Eva had made a new rule that the children could only go to the lake if they all went together. Once they were at the lake area, everybody had to stay together to ensure they all were supervised and got home safely. All the children agreed to this with no hesitation. At nine o'clock at night, all the children had to be in their rooms so Paul and Eva could make one last round to make sure everyone is present.

A couple of weeks went by and no other problems occurred. The police do not have any leads at all and like the previous families' case, they are on a dead end. Paul and Eva were relieved that the remaining children seemed to be safe, but they did not trust that things would stay that way. Who knew when the next significant problem would occur?

The police department kept in touch with the family and assured them they were working hard to find their son. Every day they sent a cop to patrol the area and the mansion. Maybe whoever is responsible for this vicious attack was hidden in the woods nearby. Soon, tensions were down a little, and very slowly, family life started to resume its normal patterns at least they must; except with a missing boy.

Late one afternoon, Paul returned to the barn and started to work again in earnest to make money for the family. As he worked, he tried to figure a way to get the attention of nearby neighbors to be on the lookout for Angelo. Finally, he and Eva decided to go to the nearest church to see whether there is any chance someone there would recognize the missing boy, but there is no trace of Angelo to be found. Just like in a nightmare, he had simply disappeared. They started knocking from houses to houses showing Angelo's picture, but none had seen the boy.

CHAPTER 3

The Mysterious Discovery

The next day while he is working behind the barn not too far from the site of the supposed alien landing, Paul found something. Three enormous ants unlike anything he had ever seen before were in front of him. Closer investigation revealed the tracks of some animal that Paul is not familiar with—it had trampled the grass all around the circle as if it had been walking in a pattern. Still, there is no clue to Angelo's whereabouts. Paul had hoped to find a scrap of cloth, perhaps even a shoe—anything to lead him to the real cause of Angelo's disappearance.

Paul began to follow the trail, but abruptly turned around and went home. He loaded his revolver and then returned to the trail. He had been walking for about an hour when he suddenly heard a strange noise. His heart started to beat a little faster; it occurred to him that he is about to face the cause of his ordeal. Quietly, he squatted down, gripped, and cocked his revolver, and crawled through the underbrush. When he arrived close to the place where he believed the noise is coming from, he stood up to fire off a quick shot at the bird, holding the trigger of his pistol in the direction of the noise. This is when he realized that it's just the neighbor's dog running free and having his good old' time. Relieved that he had not pulled the trigger of his gun,

Paul decided to walk back home and check on the other children. On his way back, Paul passed by the circle in the grass and examined it a little more closely.

He found the children in the front yard getting ready to take to the lake; they had packed a tent to spend the night there. Paul told them to stay away from the circle area and to be extra careful and watchful. When Paul walked into the house, Eva is happy to see him and asked how his day had gone so far. Then she asked him, "Any signs of Angelo?"

"I am not sure, I found something not too far from the barn," Paul said. "It's something strange. I can't explain it; I am starting to see odd creatures." "Tell me—Don't make me suffer more?" Eva said "Well, during my cleanup behind the barn, I found three big ants—I have never seen anything that big before."

"Did you touch them?" Eva asked, looking frightened, "I don't want to lose you too. Remember, the blackbird swoops down and pecks on you too."

"No, I did not touch any of them, and I told the children to stay out of that area," Paul said. "If you are done eating, we could go there together," Eva said. Paul agreed and went to eat the snack Eva had prepared for him. He had not realized how hungry he was until then.

After he finished eating, Paul and Eva hurried outside and headed in the direction of the discovery. There is a dead insect, and they examined the creature closely. They decided that it was not an ant, but something that looked like one. It could have been a different insect altogether because it apparently had been dead for a long time.

"Well, dear," Paul said, "I guess I will call the police and leave this in their hands—see what they can come up with."

Eva agreed, and they decided to walk by the lake to check on their children. Their tents were quiet, and the children were sleeping peacefully, all bundled together. Once he and Eva were on their way home, Paul picked up the phone and called the police department to report the mysterious discovery. Two officers soon arrived, and they walked to the scene with Paul and Eva. After a close look, they consulted with a lab technician and removed samples from the area. The police wanted to leave the ant whole, as they considered it a crime scene investigation. The police took pictures and measurements and marked off the place with yellow tape that said, "Do Not Remove".

Then they headed back to the house, and on their way, the policemen chatted about their jobs and how busy they were. Then, one of the men asked Paul and Eva if anything strange had happened lately.

"No, sir, nothing new happened," Paul said. "Hope it stays like that." "Where are the children?" the officer asked, looking around.

"They're all taking nap by the lake, their favorite place," Eva said. "It has been a couple of weeks now and nothing bad happened we just can't deprive our children summer good time."

The policeman looked surprised and replied, "Be careful—just tell your kids to be careful always."

"Oh, we gave them some rules," Paul said. "We told them that if they didn't follow those rules, they would never set foot in the lake again."

With that, the police were on their way back to their precinct. Paul and Eva sat down at the kitchen table, enjoying a fresh cup of coffee.

Soon enough the children were to be seen running around the lake like little rabbits, laughing and making a lot of happy noise. Eva had begun preparing a little snack so when the children arrived, they could have a warm meal. The children ran back to the house, saying they had had a wonderful night. "For the first time, we built a little fire and told spooky stories, and we had no problem with it," Alex said. "Whatever happened to Angelo won't happen again—we're sure."

Paul and Eva were happy that their children were more confident about staying because the lake offered those good times and adventures all the ways through summer vacation. Still, the parents reminded their children to be aware of their surroundings and keep a sharp eye open for anything unusual. To that, Alex replied, "Yes, sure, we'll be careful. You can count on us." Paul is determined to get Angelo back; he knows he cannot count on the police. So, he tried researching about the previous families who lived at the mansion. He tried looking for old newspapers. He found them all, all cold cases and the police have nothing. Absolutely nothing! He does not want it to happen to his son's case.

The week is coming to an end, and the Sunday housewarming party is still on schedule. They were looking forward to hosting other members of the family and celebrating the move with them. They had already received some RSVPs—even more than they had expected. One is from a previous owner of the mansion who invited himself. Paul and Eva were anxious to ask him some questions of interest.

In the meantime, the cleanup of the house and property, for the most part, is finished. The one thing Paul had not had time to do is to try to move the loader. After all, he really did not need it because the tractor never gave him a hard time again after the tire problem. Paul kept a positive attitude that he would finish up the outside of the mansion cleanup work before Friday night. It is already Wednesday, and that gave him only two days to wrap up work and put all his equipment back into the garage and the barn.

Eva, meanwhile, is busy preparing food, decorations, and a welcome sign to be posted on the street so members of the family would not have a hard time finding the mansion. Everything is running smoothly, and even the police that was sent to patrol the mansion noticed and commented on the progress Paul and Eva had made.

"Just a couple of little details, and we'll be all set for the housewarming party," Paul said. After putting everything back in its place—tools, tractor, and pick up—Paul walked back to the house and sat down in the kitchen with Eva. They had begun to relax a little bit because they had not seen the blackbird lately, and nothing else had happened since Angelo's sad disappearance. They worried, however, about how they would tell the rest of the family about the boy's disappearance; especially because the details were so sketchy. They considered many options, but none of them seemed quite right, so they reflected on the subject and decided to give themselves a couple of more hours to come to a decision.

The children were excited about Saturday—they were looking forward to seeing all their friends and relatives. In fact, they had planned their own festive welcome for the housewarming party; their parents did not know anything about it, so it would be a surprise for them also. The children guarded their big secret carefully and were pleased with their own innovation and creativity. "We can't tell Mom and Dad," they whispered to each other, "Because they might be too protective and not allow us to go through with it." They also worried about deceiving their parents, so at the last minute, they decided to tell them.

"Mom, Dad—we wanted to let you know that we made some special plans for the housewarming party," Patrick, another boy, said. Paul and Eva were pleased but concerned; Paul asked about the details and if the "plans" were close to the restricted area. "No," Patrick replied, "Far from it. They have nothing to do with that area—not even close to it."

"Okay," Paul said. "You can go ahead with your plans to welcome all your little friends. Remember, before you go too far out into the wooded area, we want you to tell us, so an adult is there to look after you."

The children promised that they would abide by the rules and that they would let their parents know before even going to explore the rest of the property. The children were pleased that their parents had not imposed too many restrictions and limits—so pleased that they all got together near the lake one evening to put the final touches on their plans. That night, the children gathered around the campfire as usual, joking, laughing, and running around. They chattered excitedly about their plans and the sure success of their very own welcome party.

In the meantime, the parents were upset; They cannot stop thinking about Angelo, he should have been here busy planning the surprise. They had counted on their children to keep the secret about the mysterious disappearance of Angelo. Their children' imaginative plan would help forestall an immediate revelation about the tragedy. Paul and Eva were already discussing what to tell the children to say if questions about Angelo arose. The problem is that they did not want their children to learn how to lie, but this situation is hard to deal with. Finally, after long thought, the parents came up with an excellent plan: They would say that Angelo had been sent to visit another relative who cannot make it to the party.

With this plan in place, Paul and Eva walked to the lake to talk to their children, telling them that their plan is best for everyone. The children all agreed to abide by their parents' wishes; they knew how much their parents were hurting and dreaming about their son. They shared their parents' pain, because they too, missed Angelo. The mystery of his disappearance is still raw for them too.

With the last preparations underway, there is just one crucial detail left to complete the family's plans. They knew that the police would be present during the housewarming party, and it would be hard to explain why.

Paul and Eva gave long thought about the problem but just could not come up with a good answer. On the one hand, they wanted their children to be safe. They knew it is possible that any of them could be targeted at any time. On the other hand, the rest of the family would certainly ask why the police were present. The situation is getting harder and harder for Paul each day, they could not control the police department and tell them what to do.

Finally, Paul said to Eva, "Well, my dear, let me deal with this one. Give me until the end of the day and will come up with some solution." Eva agreed and resumed her busy schedule, making sure that all the food would be on time and well-prepared.

As a precaution, Eva had hidden all the saltshakers because she remembered the first meal she had served in the mansion and did not want to have another bad surprise. Then, she called the locksmith and asked if he had time to install a lock on the kitchen door. "Sure," he said. "I'll get it done for you. When do you need it?"

"As soon as possible," Eva replied. "I am expecting a lot of company this weekend, and I can't go without it."

"Well, today's Friday," he said. "I have got a couple of things to finish, and I will be right over."

Eva felt more relaxed and happier now that she had gotten one of her prime concerns taken care of. In the meantime, Paul is still working on the place and trying to think up a solution to a problem at the same time. How could he disguise the police patrol on his property during the housewarming party?

Paul wanted to move the big loader out of the barn. Approaching the barn, he suddenly remembered that this is the exact place where the blackbird had swooped down and pecked at Angelo's head, as well as his. As a precaution, he walked back to the house, grabbed his revolver, and then walked back to the barn. Feeling more secure, he opened the barn door and walked directly toward the loader. It is a Volvo, and new looking. The hydraulic system appeared to be in good condition, and the hoses were of good quality; he did not foresee any major problems. He checked the tire pressure and fuel levels—everything seemed okay and ready to go. So, without hesitation, he turned the key in the ignition. The lights came on; the battery had kept the charge. He turned the key further and cranked the motor, and after a couple of tries, he had the motor started.

Pleased, he stepped down from the loader and looked around, making sure nothing would be in his way when he backed up the big machine. Then he climbed back onto the seat and engaged the transmission, recalling the pickup transmission problem as he did so. This went very smoothly. With a sense of relief, he moved his foot onto the clutch, and the Volvo is backing out of the barn.

The children, finally finishing up their secret plans, realized that their dad had moved the loader out of the barn. They all ran to see it because it is the first time, he had ever moved the machine. Full of excitement, all the children jumped onto the inside bucket, cheering like little football players after the game-winning touchdown. Paul engaged the emergency brake and walked back to the barn to close the door. He is proud to see his children so happy, but he and Eva would be happier if the children are all complete.

After a little while, the children jumped off the bucket and ran into the house, excited to see the big machine up and running. Paul had a lot on his mind, but he cherished that moment. He wiped away a tear as he thought about his missing son. "If only Angelo were here," Paul said quietly to himself. "He would have been thrilled—he loves this kind of thing."

The night is drawing near, and soon they would be celebrating their new home with their extended family. Still, the problem with the police is haunting him. What can I do? Paul kept repeating. What can I do? I just cannot seem to come up with a plan, and I know Eva is expecting an answer.

By late Friday night, Paul finally had a plan. He sat down to tell Eva about it. "Well, my dear, I think I have found a solution—this one will work only if the police department agrees with it." He stated that after long thought, he had decided that the police should dress as normal civilians. Of course, that would involve some compromises.

Eva liked the idea and appeared very encouraged. This solution seemed to be the most realistic one. "Keep going," she said. "It sounds like a really good plan so far."

Paul said, "Well, let us call the police department to see if this is even possible. We would have to treat the undercover policeman like a really close friend so the other members of the family wouldn't suspect that anything is wrong." "Not a bad idea," Eva said, smiling.

Paul replied, "You know, my dear, when you let a problem floating around in your mind awhile and think about it seriously, eventually the solution comes." Without waiting another moment, Paul grabbed the phone and dialed the number for the police precinct. "Police department," said the voice on the other end. As Paul started to respond, the officer said, "Ho! I know who you are. How are things going for you?"

"Well, just fine, I guess," Paul replied. "Nothing special is going on—the same old thing. I have not found my son yet and I am extremely upset and anxious about this whole situation. Rest assured as you know, I am still looking for him. By the way, do you have any results from the laboratory concerning those strange ants?" "Not yet," the officer said. "We're still working on it. Like everything, it takes time to solve mysteries; especially with a case like yours."

"Thank you—at least something is being done about it," Paul said. "The reason I am calling is that we're having a housewarming party to celebrate our new home, and we have invited family and friends. As of now, we are expecting about two hundred and fifty people. I am hoping to keep Angelo's disappearance a secret as much as possible."

"I don't blame you for that," the officer replied. "The fewer people involved in situations like this, the better for speeding up the case."

"Thank you, sir," Paul said. "As always, I know I can count on you. Now, here is my dilemma: I know that officers are patrolling my house and property twenty-four hours a day, but I just feel uncomfortable having officers in full uniform here during the housewarming party."

"That makes sense. How about we dress like civilians for the day?"

Paul loved that the policeman initiated the proposition and is pleased to see that it would be possible. "Sounds like a good plan," he said. It is a big relief for him because he had had the problem on his mind all day and part of the night. Having this strategy in place is good news after a week of hard work and suffering through unexpected problems.

Sitting by the phone in the mansion, Paul is visibly relieved and calm. For now, everything is under control. As responsible parents, he and Eva did want their children to enjoy the housewarming party, knowing that one of their brothers is missing. Not a day went by when Angelo's name was not mentioned and when some remembrance of him did not take place. Paul and Eva had already set up appointments for their children to get counseling to help them cope with the cruel reality of Angelo's disappearance. It is as if Angelo had been chosen by an evil spirit—yet another victim of this mansion... yet another boy who had vanished without leaving a trace.

Eva had been standing there with an expectant look on her face since Paul had hung up the phone. "Do you have any good news?" she asked.

"Yes, I do," Paul said proudly. "I didn't even need to make the proposition—the officer brought up the idea himself. I couldn't believe it!"

"Are we still on with the rest of the plans that we came up with for the housewarming party?"

"I guess we are because after all, these officers will be part of us until we recover our son. I have this feeling that one day we will see Angelo again; I also know that anything can happen until he is finally rescued. Where he is now, I do not have a clue, but I do know something. If I do not give up and I continue to believe that everything will be alright, even if everything seems to be going against me time after time, I – we can make this. Sooner or later things will fall into place.

How many times have you heard a story about a child who has gone missing? I have heard those stories several times, but I never thought that it would happen to us; to our child. Time is ticking dear; every hour and day means the slimmer the chance we have on finding him."

Eva nodded solemnly. She offered some coffee and cookies to Paul, and then she went about her last-minute duties of preparation. Paul walked around the house to make sure that all the doors were locked in the night.

Finally, Paul and Eva were ready for the big event, where family and friends would be gathering at the housewarming party and reunion.

CHAPTER 4

The Family reunion

Saturday morning brought the early birds and their families. The first to arrive is the previous owner of the mansion. At first, Paul is not too happy about the fact that the former owner, who had invited himself, is first one pulling up to the mansion. But after thinking about it, he changed his attitude. This might be a good way to befriend the guy and ask him some questions, he thought.

The man is sitting at the same table with Paul, having breakfast and a fresh cup of coffee. Paul asked the former owner his name and noticed that the man seemed extremely cautious, weighing every word, making Paul skeptical. The former owner replied, "My name is Harry. It is nice to meet you. What's your name?" Paul gave him his name and the conversation fell into the mansion. Paul asked the former owner some brief questions. From his answers, Paul discovered that Yes, this guy obviously knows something.

As other people arrived, Paul became distracted and lost track of the previous owner. The phone rang; it was his brother, calling from the road. He said a black object had come out of the air and hit his car, and not too long afterward, he had a flat tire. "Oh no," said Paul. "Wait. You saw something flying?" "Yes, I am telling you, something definitely flew our way. The children saw it happened too."

Paul's heart began to pound. "Don't move," he said. "I will be right there." "You don't need to panic," his brother said. "It's just a little flat—I just need your help changing the tire. I am not too far away from your place."

"Sure, I will be right there. Sorry if I got a little nervous. See you soon." Paul jumped into the pickup, and soon he is on the road, driving to the rescue of his brother Ron and his family. There is only one thing on Paul's mind, and that is avoiding the curse that seemed to follow his family right after they moved. I will have to make sure nothing bad happens to one of his children. Otherwise, I will never hear the end of it. He drove for a few miles until he saw his brother's car in the distance and pulled over to the side of the road. As he drove closer, he could almost sense a presence in the air, but he decided that it was just his fertile imagination. He pulled up in front of his brother's car. Together the two men lifted the car, exchanged the flat tire for the spare, and then examined the flat closely. It is slashed, just as Paul's tire had been, and with the same precision. He could not believe his eyes. "My God!" he exclaimed, thinking, this is too much of a similarity. "Are you sure that your tire is in perfect condition before the trip?"

"Yes, I am telling you, bro. You know me—I have always taken good care of my car and truck. Why would I change now?"

Paul did not answer; he just walked back to the pickup. As he sped back home, Paul called Eva from the road to tell her what had happened. "You know, I really believe that they're after us," he said. "Why didn't anyone else on that road have a flat tire, and only my brother? Look, there must be at least seventy-five cars in our yard and only Ron had a flat on their way up here."

His brother arrived home right behind him, and Paul asked him to park close to the house so that he could keep an eye on his car while he is out having a good time.

"Good. It'll be nice to park right next to the house, so I won't have to walk too far," his brother said.

By now all the guests had greeted each other and had begun touring the property. The children all walked together toward the lake and soon they were pitching their tents for the night. As for the mansion's previous owner, no one knew his of his were about. Paul is a little unnerved by this He glanced at all the cars and realized that the man's car is gone. While Paul is busy welcoming his brother and finding a parking place for him, he had lost track of where the ex-owner is and what he is doing. Things had started to flow, and the party is in full swing when Paul suddenly realized that his sister had not shown up yet.

He went back into the house, where Eva is busy getting things ready in the kitchen. "Have you heard any word from my sister? She should have been here by now," he said.

"No," Eva said and then forced a smile. "That sounds strange to me. She's the one who never let you down and is always by your side from the day I met you."

Worried, Paul said, "Maybe she will be in soon. Maybe she stopped at the store to get something. That would be the best scenario."

Suddenly the phone rang; it was his sister. Paul answered anxiously. "Hello there! How are things going for you? Where are you? Why aren't you here yet?"

She replied, "Well, I am not too terribly far away, I think I am having transmission problems. My car just stopped, and now it will not go anywhere. I am parked beside a gravel road."

"I will be right over," Paul said. "Do you think you're low on transmission fluid?"

"I am not sure. The only thing I know is that there is a lake of something under the car."

"Boy, that's not good news. Be patient—I need to go to the store and buy some transmission and motor fluid and then I will be right with you. It will not be long. I am sorry that you're stuck." Paul hung up the phone and wiped his forehead with his hand. He is frustrated and could not believe what is happening. Without saying anything to Eva, he walked back to the pickup.

Paul drove to the store and bought some transmission fluid, motor oil, a filter, a funnel, and a couple of rags. Then he is on his way to help his sister. Driving carefully, he sensed heaviness in the atmosphere again at the very same place where he had come to the rescue of his brother. I will notify the police department tomorrow, he thought. Will they believe me is I say that the mansion is cursed?

His imagination is running wild the entire time before he reached his sister, who is sitting in her stalled car on the side of the gravel road. Paul immediately noticed the spreading puddle beneath the car. Yes, this might be a big problem. He opened the hood and checked the oil, which is fine. Then he checked the transmission fluid: empty. Wow, Paul thought. This is too much of a coincidence. First, my brother has a flat tire—ironically, on the same side of the vehicle as mine—and now all my sister's transmission fluid overflows. With his thoughts racing, Paul added transmission fluid and then asked his sister to try to make the car move. It is a success: the car is moving. Paul told her to drive ahead of him so he could follow her back to his house. She waited for her brother to get into his pickup, and soon they were on their way.

Barely five minutes later, had the car stalled again. Paul's nerves were frayed, and he felt like a major breakdown is imminent. For his sister's sake, he managed to keep his cool. He walked to her car again to see what the problem might be, murmuring, "I hope this is not another overflow of transmission fluid. That would only prove to me that my immediate family is not the only target—my brother and sister are cursed too." When he flipped the hood up, his fears were confirmed.

Given the fact that the transmission is overflowing without any reason, Paul almost told his sister that he would just take her home and they would forget about the housewarming party. But he realized that he could not do that without jeopardizing all his and Eva's hard work. Plus, he would be spoiling the good time for his family and friends who had already gathered. So, he just kept quiet and started to siphon off the excess fluid.

Meanwhile, Eva had begun to worry about Paul and asked Ron to go check on him. Paul had been gone two hours already and should have been back a long time ago. She is wondering if something horrible had taken place. Ron accepted and he was also worried, recalling his own bad experience on his way up. Within minutes, he is in his car after having checked his tire pressure. Along the way, he felt an uncomfortable feeling right where Paul had, but he paid no attention to it. After all, he did not know the whole story.

He had a strange feeling about the place after a blackbird hit his car there and he had gotten a flat tire.

When he arrived at the scene Ron saw his brother looking under the hood of his sister's car. Ron thought, must be the motor. He hurried over, wondering what the problem might be. He knew that their sister had recently had maintenance done on the car—he knew because he had driven the car to the garage himself. "What's going on here?" he asked. Paul, preoccupied with worry, did not answer.

Joanne steps out of the car to greet her brother. Then she asked him if he truly had driven the car to the garage the day before. "I hope you didn't play a dirty joke on me," she said. Offended, he replied, "You know I would never do anything like that to you."

"I know," Joanne said. "But I thought maybe you did something just to be funny. You do things like that from time to time." "Oh no, not at all," he replied.

"Are you kidding me?" she said, shaking her head. Then she turned to Paul. "Well, something is obviously going on here. You're not usually quiet unless you have a problem."

"I am as puzzled as you are," Paul responded. "I don't understand this situation at all." Paul is trying to keep his cool because he was not good at keeping secrets. Yet, he did not want to sound an alarm that could wreck the day for all the other friends and family having a good time. When Paul had finished working on the transmission, the fluid is back to a normal level. He held his breath for a minute then closed the hood. "Let us go home," he said, "and enjoy the rest of the day."

They all returned to their cars and drove the rest of the way without an incident—except that at the same place along the road, the mysterious presence still made itself known to both Paul and his brother. Ron is following Paul closely, which allowed them to notice each other's reactions in that specific area of the road.

All three cars arrived at the mansion at the same time. They were relieved that nothing else bad had happened and that the negative experiences they had had were not expensive ones. Eva is relieved to see that everyone is okay. She rushed over to Paul, asking, "What took so long? Did something happen?"

Paul took her aside and explained what had happened, assuring her that he had everything covered. "No one knows anything about Angelo yet," he said, "I am not sure if Ron believes me that there is nothing strange going on." Paul knew that his brother, a lawyer, was far from being uneducated. Paul is banking on the chance that he had not yet realized that there is anything wrong. In fact, if his brother had sensed a problem, he would have asked Paul about it outright—or maybe he is just waiting for more proof. Paul is counting on that being the case; he had not doubted it given his brother's intelligence and intuition. All he could do is hope.

Suddenly, something had his attention; it was the mansion's former owner, who had come back and was getting out of his car. Something about it did not look right to Paul. "The entire time you were out trying to get your sister to the housewarming party, he was nowhere to be seen," said Eva. Now, not even half an hour after they all arrived back, here he is again, pulling in. I have got to talk to the guy, Paul said to himself firmly. Joining his thoughts with action, he walked up to the man. "Harry, can I have a few minutes please?"

"Sure. What's up?"

"Well," Paul said, "I know you're one of the former owners of the place here, Harry. I just have a question to ask."

"Go right ahead. I am all yours. I hope I can be of help to you know the former owner just before you did the same thing. I believe I know what you want to talk about."

Paul is more relaxed now that he knew that the man is willing to talk. "Did you have any bad things happen to you here?"

"Well, let's see," Harry said. "All kinds of things happened here, but no one is tenacious enough to get to the bottom of them." He looked at Paul for a moment and then added, "Looking at you and judging your persistence I believe that you are strong enough to solve the mystery that this place holds."

Pau reassured that he is telling the truth, pressed on. "What mysteries are you talking about? Is this place haunted or cursed? I am starting to feel that you know?"

"Of course, I do. I was forced to keep them to myself because everyone left the place before I could talk to them. Are you willing to stay here and see this through?"

"I am ready," Paul said. "I am more than ready if you can help me solve this problem—after all, my family loved it here."

"Yes, I know. I used to say the same thing myself, but after a while, I could not take it anymore. This is what gives me confidence in you—the fact that you've stayed the course up until now."

By now, Paul knew that the man is sincere, but somehow, he just could not trust him entirely. "Where did you go earlier?" he asked. "I know you were the first one here this morning, and then I lost you. Now that my sister, brother, and I are here, you appear again."

"I don't live far from here," Harry said, "but I don't give out my address. The reason I do not like to give out my address is that previously I was accused of doing bad things that I did not do. You know, I am not the type of person who would take pleasure in physically or mentally torturing someone else. Some people left this place, and even today they blame me for events and mysteries that happened here a long time ago."

The conversation had taken an interesting and critical turn. Paul wanted to know more, so he did not say anything but just listened to what the man had to say.

"I know that this place has been possessed by some strange force, and I do believe that I have the key to establishing peace again. But for this to happen, you have to be patient."

At this point, Paul said, "You know something about this place. Could you tell me what it is? I promise you I will keep this a secret between you and me."

Harry looked into Paul's eyes and replied, "I know you are not like the rest because you're the first one to talk to me like this. You know, all the other former owners wanted to kill me, and therefore I decided to hide not too far from here. I do not know how many times I have saved them from bigger trouble. I have tried to tell them, but they were so angry that they did not want to listen to me. Instead, they blamed me."

Paul thought the conversation is at a turning point. Maybe he can tell me where Angelo is; how he vanished without a trace.

"Are you aware that people have been disappearing mysteriously from this mansion?" Paul asked.

"Of course, I am. That is why I have had fingers pointed at me and have been blamed for these monstrous crimes. But I swear I didn't have anything to do with them."

"But do you clue where to look, what steps to take to find them?" "Yes," Harry said. "But if I tell you, you must keep it secret—and don't turn me into the police. I am telling you these things because I have tried to help others, but it only came back to bite me."

Paul, realizing that he might be on the way to recovering his son, quickly reassured him. "You can count on me. I understand your situation and the fragility of the matter. What more can you tell me about these cases? I have a great interest in solving them myself."

"You know," Harry said, "I am going to lead you through it step-by-step, it's a complex situation Paul. I am not sure if you will believe me, but I guess you do not have any choice. If you trust me and follow all my advice, I am sure you will find answers to all your questions. "Paul now knew that his son is alive somewhere, and that patience is the key to recovering him.

"First, you have to pay very close attention," Harry said. "Pay attention to every single clue, no matter how small and insignificant it might look. It could be something as small as a piece of paper telling you what your next step should be. Second, the clues could involve common things, things we use daily. Third, in this case, no small evidence can be ignored. Do you hear me?"

"Yes," Paul said. "I am all ears, tell me what to do." Then he walked away for a little while, joining family and friends gathered for the housewarming party. After a few moments Harry the former owner followed Paul into the house. "I forgot to tell you something," he said. "Look for a cave." Paul reached for a sheet of paper lying on the living room table and wrote that down, along with notes from his conversation with Harry, hoping that they could lead him and the investigators to a potential clue.

The children, who were all hanging out together, were almost done eating. They asked Paul if they could spend some time at the lake and perhaps go fishing. They promised to stay together and not be too wild. Paul told them they could. Then, he went to talk to the undercover policeman and told him that the children were on their way to the lake. Quickly, the policeman left the house to follow behind them, surveying the area along the way. Most of the children did not even notice him because they were having so much fun.

Eva, who had been hard at work in the kitchen, finally joined the party, relieved that nothing else bad had happened and that the day is going as planned. The adults were touring the grounds, visiting the barn, the garage, and the house itself. They were all happy and proud of Paul and Eva because the mansion is huge, and it looked very elegant.

Paul spent some of his time in the barn, busily ensuring that no one enters there, he made sure that everything in it was protected from family and friends walking through. He is not done with the barn yet, not yet! He is sensing something of interest in there, but he cannot figure what it is, do not know what it is. There goes this funny feeling again. As he worked, he reflected on the conversation he had just had with the home's previous owner. Maybe he is a good man, after all, Paul thought. Maybe I just misjudged him at first. I the police told me to be on the lookout for one of the former owners, could it be him? Anyway, he was glad that he had decided to stay put, talking to Harry somehow gives him the hope that Angelo is still alive and well.

By now everyone at the housewarming party had found something to do. Family members came by the barn to examine Paul's new loader, tractor, and pickup. As time went by, everyone looked relaxed and comfortable. No one suspected the ordeal that the family had been through.

After a while, Eva found a chance to talk to Paul alone. "What did you and Harry talk about?" she asked. "I noticed you and Harry spoke for a long time."

"We'll talk about it later—now isn't a good time," he said. "But I will say that there is a lot of good news." Elated that her husband is onto something, Eva looked radiant but said nothing further.

As they stood together in the barn, Paul's brother came up to them and put his arm around him. "I am so proud of you," he said. "This is like a dream come true. I know that you looked for a long time for something like this and that you put in a lot of time and made a lot of sacrifices to finally acquire your life's dream."

"You're right, bro," Paul said. "And I really appreciate the fact that you recognize my efforts. You know, nowadays people tend to be jealous of what others have. They forget about the long hours of work and saving that went into it, and only judge people by what they see."

Paul looked around, smiling. "One day this place will be a paradise—and that will come from a lot of patience, faith, and love. Integrity and resourcefulness are particularly important to me because I have learned that you have to walk a hard road before you can start to relax and enjoy yourself."

Then they all stepped out of the barn. It is a perfect, sunny day, neither too hot nor too cold. Some visiting family members had bought fireworks for later that night, and already the children had made some excursions and were thrilled by the beautiful lake and beach. Some of them decided they wanted to climb the mountain, so they made the proposal to the other children. Soon all the children were clamoring to go. They finally convinced Alex, one of Paul and Eva's sons, to go ask his dad to okay the plan. "You know, Dad," he said, "we've been here for three months now, and we've never had a chance to climb that mountain."

Paul is skeptical. "I am not too confident about letting you all climb that mountain," he said.

"Oh, come on, Dad. Please let us go! We want to explore it. Maybe there's a lake on top... or even a gold mine!"

Paul wanted to say yes, but the trauma of having lost Angelo is just too fresh. The other children stood quietly, holding their breath because they knew that it would not be easy to get Paul's permission. It is a hard decision to make. What terrible thing could happen if I let them go? Paul wondered. Will they all return safely to their families? He told his son that he needed some time to think about it, and to come back to him in a couple of hours. Alex went back to the lake and told the others that Paul had asked for a couple of hours to decide. They all nodded, keeping their hopes high because they really wanted to explore that part of the paradise.

Paul stayed near the barn and guarded it because he felt sure that a major clue would be there somewhere. He weighed the pros and cons of letting the children have an adventure on the mountain.

What to do? He thought. I cannot deprive these children of climbing the mountain and have a good time. Well, I still have an hour to make up my mind. One thought kept floating into his mind; it is about the cave Harry told Paul about. This would be the perfect time to send the children to the mountain, where they could have safety in numbers and enjoy supervised fun. And maybe they would find the cave.

If this cave is discovered, Paul thought, I might be closer to where my son is. On the other hand, he is afraid and reluctant. What if they found the cave and more children disappeared? Paul realized that he had to take the chance now or wait until he could explore the mountain himself—and between his work and the upkeep of the mansion, he did not have the time. The time off from the housewarming party was a good time for Paul to explore the rest of the property and he decided that letting the children go is a good idea after all. Paul walked back to where the rest of the adults were finishing eating. He mentioned that the children wanted to climb the mountain and that he thought it would be a good exercise for them. The rest of the adults approved with no objections; some even offered to go with the children to explore the beautiful mountain. The ones who were willing and young enough to make the climb got together and walked to the lake. The children, seeing some of the other adults coming their way, were happy because they could ask for permission again to climb the mountain. When the adults announced that they were willing to go with the children a happy yell is heard from the children and they ran to their tents to put on their running shoes in preparation. The adults patiently waited for them on the beach. Soon all the children were ready, laughing and giggling in their excitement.

Paul joined the group after a moment in the house, where he had gone to grab a little notebook and a pen to take notes with. He also took a couple of lanterns in case they found a cave. As he left the house, Eva said to him, "Be careful. Don't tell them anything."

"Don't worry, my dear," Paul said. "As of now, no one has a clue." No one had asked where Angelo is or what had happened to him, so Paul and Eva felt that everything would be all right. "I love you," Eva said, giving Paul a big hug.

"I love you too," he said. "We'll be back soon." With that, he rushed toward the lake knowing the others were already starting to walk towards the mountain. When he reached the group, he talked to them and gave lanterns to the adults who believed his hypothesis that there is a hidden cave in the mountain.

It took about half an hour to get to the foot of the mountain; the children were so excited that they had run nearly the whole way. Before they began climbing, they stopped and gathered around Paul, who gave his instructions and recommended that everyone stay together—especially the children, who were to stay within sight of the adults. These were the conditions, he said, and everyone had to comply, no exceptions.

All the children responded obediently. "Yes sir," they said. "Now can we start to climb the mountain?" "Yes, you may." The first thing Paul noticed is a trail—not fresh, but still visible. It is as if someone had already been here, and not too long ago. Paul is a little scared. Maybe this is not a good idea after all. Then again, maybe my son is here somewhere.

He went along with the group despite his anxiety, and nothing abnormal happened—no signs of Angelo. His heart is pounding, and he is feeling uneasy as the former owner's words "look for a cave," went round and round in his head. Paul tried to subdue his fear; he did not want the rest of the group to sense it. The energy flowing from the adults and children is boundless, and the group is following the little trail to wherever it led. About three-quarters of the way up the mountain, they discovered a lake whose water is so pure and crystalline that its sun-dappled surface looked like millions of twinkling diamonds. The group spent a long time admiring the charming natural panorama. Suddenly, several big fish jumped out of the clear water to dive right back in, forming a little rainbow lit by the sun's reflection. It is a beautiful sight, and many of the adults commented that they would love to own such a lake.

CHAPTER 5

The Cave

With everyone staying together, the group finally resumed their exploration of the mountain—though the children were too busy running, jumping across streams, or walking on fallen logs to make any real discoveries. Before long, however, some of the children stopped to stare at some strange ants. The insects were so big that the children could not believe what they were seeing.

They alerted the adults, and soon everyone in the group had gathered around to see this new point of interest. Coming up behind them, Paul took out his notebook and made a note of the location, have decided to write down anything that might be able to help him find his lost son. When he peered over their shoulders to take in the scene, he almost dropped his notebook. He is in a state of shock. It is too much of a coincidence, and he genuinely believed he is just about to find his lost son. The others took great interest in the size of the ants—monsters they were, for sure.

The children had cornered some of the ants and wanted to pick them up, but everyone opposed the idea, so the children let them go. Anyway, they could not keep the insects because no one had brought a container—except Paul, who had thought of it after his conversation about clues with the mansion's former owner.

After the group moved on, Paul carefully pulled a plastic container out of his back pocket and with the lid, captured a couple of the ants. Then, he continued the discovery phase of his journey. No one had noticed Paul picking up these ants, and Paul is counting on that fact to help him cover up the real reason he is with them on the mountain.

Farther up the trail, another interesting detail emerged, one that almost gave Paul a heart attack. They came to a crossroads where the trail divided into two paths like a "Y". There is no sign for one of the paths, but a sign for the other is shaped like an arrow. The sign shaped like an arrow read, "Blackbird Trail This Way".

Paul is lagging the group, by now he is busy taking notes and marking trees so he could make an easy return at another time with a police officer. By the time he caught up with the rest of the group at the crossroads, his thoughts were running wild. The other adults could see that he is agitated about something, but they decided to leave him alone.

The adults consulted with one another about which direction to take, finally deciding to flip a coin. Head up and they would take Blackbird Trail and tails up they would take the alternate path. At this point, Paul is hoping that the coin would fall on "tails" because the least that he wanted now is another trouble, now that all the children are here, all he knew I if the blackbird is around something is going to happen. Please not now! Paul thought.

He had a family to provide for, so he is not too anxious to go further. But, because of his last conversation with the house's former owner, he decided to continue the adventure. Harry had said that Paul had to follow every clue to resolve the problem and that it would take a strong person to get to the bottom of it all. He also told Paul that he is the one who could solve it. The coin landed on heads and Paul rushed after the rest of the group, feverish to get to the end of this trail.

Strait a head of the excursioners appeared the cave Harry had mentioned earlier to Paul. Yes! I am on the right path, Paul said to himself. Paul now genuinely believed that Harry really knew something and was trying to help. Paul marked the trees along the trail and reached in his back pocket to make sure that his notebook is still there.

The Cave

As they walked closer to the cave, Paul demanded that everybody stay together and reminded the children that hiding and running around were not allowed. He is a clever father; he had made sure that all the lanterns were properly working, and he had brought extra matches in case any of them malfunctioned. Filled with anticipation, they took the first few steps into the cave, immediately noticing that it had several levels and possibly some hidden rooms. So, they stopped and chose one—and only one—level to follow, making sure no one is left behind. No one knew how expansive or deep the cave is, so they were extremely cautious in exploring it.

As for Paul, he is constantly expecting the blackbird to show up and play the poop trick on him again. Paul is feeling more at ease that he has not seen the blackbird for days. He had become preoccupied with taking notes in his notebook when suddenly, someone exclaimed, "Look at that bird!"

Paul looked up to see the big blackbird just overhead. He dropped his pen and exclaimed breathlessly, "Oh no, this is for real! I am in the place of my torturers." Then he said to him in a low voice, "I just hope I brought my revolver with me." He did not want to kill the blackbird; he just wanted to wound it so he could take it to the police station as evidence.

The blackbird made two or three turns and then disappeared without a trace. "Wow!" said one adult, laughing. "That alone is worth coming here for. Let us see what else we can find."

Paul, on the other hand, is nervous, regretting that he had proposed climbing the mountain at all. But he realized that he is onto something and persisted for the love of his lost son. Maybe, like the mansion's former owner said, this would be the beginning of new, happier days. Could it be possible that he would rescue his son in just a matter of time? He dearly hoped so.

Suddenly, the group noticed some letters starting to appear on the wall of the cave. They were capital letters, with plenty of space between them. Paul retrieved his notebook and started to take notes and measurements, gathering evidence for the criminal investigation that he hoped to conclude when he returned home. Allowing his gaze to sweep the cave wall, he found what appeared to be the first letter:

C. The next is an A, then an R, followed by an E and an F. He shined his lantern on the wall, making out each letter and writing it: U, L, L, Y, L, O, O, K, I, N, T, H, E, B, A, R, N. The letters were spaced so far apart that some of the group wondered if what they came up with—Carefully look in the barn—is the right sentence. Surely it is something like that. Paul, of course, knew immediately that it is a clue. Again, he recalled that the blackbird had attacked his son and him not too far from the barn. Paul found himself solving puzzles and looking for clues. The barn, the cave, the blackbird, Angelo, Harry, the gigantic ants. Everything is not making sense at all.

They continued deeper into the cave until they reached a large cavern enough for three hundred people. Space is clean, almost as if someone or something had kept it neat and pleasant.

Quite some time had gone by, and some of the adults began looking at their watches. It is already two o'clock, so they decided that by three o'clock they should consider going back to the mansion. They were having such a good time and were so interested in their discoveries, not realizing that they had gone two miles into the cave. Paul, however, had only one thing on his mind. Where is my son? He wondered. Why don't you just give me back my son? Paul vowed that he would leave the blackbird alone only if it gave him some indication of where his son might be. He had had no answers so far—just a few clues to work with.

Finally, the group is satisfied with their discoveries and decided to call it a day. They turned back, finding that the walk back is a little faster. Suddenly one of the children exclaimed, "Look at this pile of poop! That was not here earlier. We must have taken the wrong way."

Several of the adults became concerned, convinced that they had lost their way, but Paul said, "No, we are on the right path. I know because I marked our way all along. I took that extra precaution because I did not want to waste time searching for the way back. After all, once our lantern oil is burned, that's it."

At that, someone said, "Let us go! We don't have a whole lot of time left with the fuel in our lanterns."

So, they picked up their speed and made their way back toward the entrance of the cave. Not before long, the big blackbird made its appearance again. Apparently, the blackbird had decided to make their exit harder, because the rock they were standing on suddenly became wet and sticky as if the glue had been poured there. The group quickly turned silent as they faced this unexpected and troubling challenge. Even the children grew quiet and wondered as they walk into the way home. For half of an hour, the group struggled through the muck. Some in the group were falling and others were holding the wall of the rock because it seemed to be the only way to keep balance. Where did this come from? they thought. Paul. Everyone had the vision of the strange black bird flying around fresh in their minds. The situation resulted in a reign of dead silence. Some of the lanterns were starting to go out creating a spooky ambiance, but the children's panic is not the answer. In the semi-darkness, they struggled to find their way out of the mess. Every step is victory and hearts beats are racing faster and faster. The children were able to find their way out easier than adults. However, the children were about to be trapped by something, scrambling for their path toward freedom. Soon enough, some of the children started to fall and the others tried to help. They were eventually all stuck to the rocks of the cave, as if by glue to the wall. Screaming, the children desperately sent signals to the adults behind them that they were in a big problem. The adults became more nervous and adamant to come to their rescue. Paul is behind the group saying, "We are fine, we are almost there okay?" As the adults were reaching toward the children, the rock started shaking violently. After a great struggle, the adults managed to free the children from the cave's sticky wall. They were not sure how long was that horrendous torment took, the good thing is all the children are free now, they started to walk out of the cave cautious enough not to get stuck or something.

The twist of events is strange and distressing, but they did not think too much about it because time is growing short and safety is their top priority. Filled with anticipation, they neared the entrance—now the exit—of the cave. They arrived at the Y intersection and finally made their way toward the sunlight. The children were running now, eager to be free of the cave and back to the mansion and the lake.

Once the group is outside, the first thing they did is make sure that everybody is accounted for. This is when they realized that Paul is missing. "Where could he possibly be?" someone asked. "We don't have much time left to wait—we need to go home." They waited for a good half hour before Paul appeared, covered in white cream. They rushed to him. "What happened to you? Oh my, that looks like a shower of poop on you. Are you all right?"

"Yes, I am all right," Paul said. "Let's get out of here." They cleaned him up the best they could and walked back to the mansion. Now Paul had some tangible clues to work with, but he is still missing some facts. Paul had just experienced something like a fistfight with the blackbird, although he failed in capturing it. Instead, he had received a shower of poop that made him blind for a while, which is why he was late leaving the cave. But now he knew that he is on the right path to recovering his lost son. How long would the rescue take? Paul did not really know, but one thing was for sure; he was more determined than ever to do it without help from anybody. Now an hour had passed since they left the cave, and everyone was together.

No one was missing, and nothing bad happened aside from that peculiar sticky rock they got stuck into. The children began running back toward the lake. Although they were exhausted from the walk, they were happy and contented about their adventure on the mountain. The adults walked back to the mansion, where the rest of the partygoers were waiting for their return. Some of the families had started to pack up because the weekend had come to an end; they had to return to work in the morning.

The adults enjoyed a good supper, talking at length about the cave that they had discovered and explored. Some of them related their own sights and experiences. Others just sat and relaxed, enjoying the evening. Paul walked into the house and went straight to the shower. After he had cleaned up, he felt rejuvenated—fresh and ready to confront the blackbird that he now knew a little more about. He knew only that this bird came from another area, possibly another planet. It was also a messenger bird just like during the old days when birds were used to transmit letters overseas.

Now that Paul knew more details, he could discuss more of the mystery with Eva and possibly speed up the investigation. He spoke briefly to the undercover policeman and then walked out to be with the rest of his family and friends. After Paul talked to him, the policeman returned to the lake, surveying the area vigilantly. He was happy that a break in the case might be on the horizon because for as long as the situation with the mansion had lasted, he had been dispatched to the same area. He is counting on peace and quiet that night so that he could consider all the new evidence and events to analyze any similarities among all the other cases related to the mansion.

Night came, and it is time for fireworks and the joyful cheers of spectators enjoying their last minutes at the mansion. Eva, meanwhile, is busy putting things back where they belonged; she had almost everything cleaned up. Eva is a highly organized person, very methodical in how she got her work done.

She brought out the last drinks of the day and sat down with the partygoers to enjoy a final visit with them. It had been years since many of the family and friends had seen each other, and it is a pleasure to connect with them again. The lively conversation went on well past midnight. The stars were shining bright, the moon is full, and the summer breeze was gentle. It is a perfect night. But her heart is heavy. She missed Angelo so much.

Eva finally went back inside and, for the first time in at least six hours, briefly to talk to her husband. "Well, did you have a good time up on the mountain?" she asked.

"My dear," replied Paul, "I have a lot of things to tell you, but you have to wait until everybody is gone."

"Oh! I hope its good news Paul, I have nothing but bad news these past weeks!" she exclaimed.

"A little bit of both," replied Paul. "But for now, why don't we focus on going to bed? It's already two o'clock, and you know we have to be up early tomorrow." She agreed, and they went to bed to recuperate from the busy day.

In the morning, the rising sun awakened most of the remaining visitors, who began packing up their belongings and making one last round to ensure they had not left anything behind. The children smothered the embers from the previous night's campfire' they also packed up their belongings and tents. They went fishing and swimming one last time, and then made their way back up to the house, stopping at the barn along the way to see the big loader and the other machinery.

When the children arrived back at the house, their families were happy to see them, and they had a good time talking about the weekend's adventures. Eva served breakfast, and then it is time for the guests to say good-bye, pack up their final belongings, and leave. For the last time, hugs and kisses were exchanged, and some of the family members were already talking about next year's reunion.

One by one the guests hit the road, and gradually the rumble of engines faded away. After two busy days, Paul and Eva finally found themselves alone with their children. They had enjoyed the company of their family and friends, but they also were happy to return to the routine of their daily life. Their children returned to the lake for a swim, with the undercover officer following along for a while to make sure that nothing bad would happen. Finally, he returned to the house to talk to Paul; he is dying to know more details of Paul's findings the day before. "What's up, man?" he asked. "Now we can finally talk and put everything on the table."

Paul called to Eva and the three of them drank cups of coffee as Paul described the many little clues and signs he had come across over the weekend. "You know, I really believe that our son is still alive," he said, "but I don't know where he could be. I am sure that resolving this will require a great deal of time and patience. I know it's a long haul, but nothing gets done in one day, and everything must come to an end—even the disappearance of our son."

"I had a notebook in my pocket, and I wrote down every little detail that I came across while I was in the cave. Now, some of my notes could be confusing because I just wrote things down as they came to me, and sometimes I did not have the proper words in my head as events were happening. I promise you that in a couple of days I will have sorted them out in greater detail, and we will be able to bust this mysterious case open. Do you remember when every day Angelo was targeted by a blackbird, the next day I became the target myself?"

"Of course, I do," Eva answered. "I dream of killing this blackbird that has disturbed us and probably stolen one of my boys."

"I know," Paul replied. "We are suffering terribly from this loss, and I can't even express the pain I feel seeing you so hurt."

The policeman took the cue and said, "Well, I think it's time for us to get busy and get things rolling again. When do think we'll have the details from your notebook?"

"As soon as possible," Paul said. "I'll try to get copied onto another sheet of paper by tomorrow for sure but give me a couple of days. I hope that's not too late."

"That's just fine," he replied. "Do you know if anyone of your family members knew that I was an undercover officer? Did anyone talk about it?"

"No, no one. Everything went well except for the first day when both my brother and my sister had some mysterious problems, like the one I had, with their cars. They arrived here simply fine, as far as I know, because I probably would have heard something by now if they hadn't." Paul had just finished the sentence when his phone rang. It was his sister Joanne. "Hello, my dear, how are things going?"

"Just fine," Joanne said. "I had no trouble whatsoever on the way home, but one strange little thing did happen."

"What is it?" he asked. "Tell me—I am dying to know." "Did you leave a note on my car?" she asked.

"No, I didn't," he said. "Someone left you a note. Where was the note left?"

"It was left on the right corner of the rear window, under the wiper arm." "Well, what did it say?" he asked, feeling a bit nervous.

"It said, 'Check the barn, the barn has a clue.'"

"That's interesting," said Paul. That just confirms my own findings, he thought. "Thanks for telling me. Could you send me the note, please?"

"Of course, I will. Other than that, nothing bad happened. We arrived home safely."

"Good," said Paul. "When do think you can send me the note?" "Don't worry, Paul, I will send it to you tomorrow. What address do you want me to put on the letter?"

Paul gave Joanne his address and they talked a little more. Then he had to go, so he hung up the phone and went back to the kitchen where Eva is still sitting at the table with the policeman. "Well, there is something new to report," he said. "My sister just called to tell me there was a note left on her rear window, under the wiper arm. It said, 'Check the barn, the barn has a clue.' Well, I am going to go through every square inch of that barn until I find that clue."

"At least you're getting somewhere," the officer said. "You're getting clues that no one else was able to get. I will let you dig for the clue in the barn—I think it is better that you search alone and look for these clues. Who knows? Maybe the responsible party is watching you see if you are being followed. I know that in my previous experiences with cases like this, we usually had more successes when the person receiving the communications handled them by himself." With this, the undercover officer said that he would go back to the precinct to report all the little facts and findings to his superiors that they had come across over the last couple of days.

"We'll call you if we need more information," he said, "or you can call us any time if anything new happens."

"Very well," said Paul. "Have a good trip back to your precinct. See you soon." The two men shook hands, and then the undercover officer is on his way. Just then the phone rang again; this time it was Paul's brother. "What is up, bro? How are things going for you?"

"Everything's fine," Alex said. "No major problems on the way home—just one disturbing thing happened."

"Well, I am curious to know what it is, but I am relieved that your tire is okay."

"Thanks, bro. You know, I think it's just a coincidence, but then again I don't think I'd be crazy to believe in paranormal stuff at this point."

"I know that bro," Paul replied. "You're not telling me anything new here. Has something happened?"

"Well, on my way home I looked through my rearview mirror and I saw that there's a note placed on my back windshield, so I pulled over to get it. It said, 'Check the barn, the barn has a clue.' Do you have any idea who would have left a note like that on the back windshield of my car?"

"I have an idea," Paul said, "but I am not sure if we are talking about the same thing. Could you mail me the note, please?"

"Yes, I will mail it to you for sure. It'll be on its way tomorrow." "Thank you," Paul said. "One more thing: can you send it as a certified letter?"

"Yes, I can do that. Why?"

"I can't tell you right now, but I promise I will one day. I will send you some money to help pay the postage."

"Don't worry about it—I was simply curious. Something sounds strange here, but I respect you and your privacy."

"Thank you, bro," Paul said. "Someday everything will be clear, I promise you." He hung up the phone.

Eva, meanwhile, had just finished the dishes. "When can we put all of this behind us?" she asked, sinking into a kitchen chair. "And when will we have our son back?"

"I don't know, my dear, but I will never give up," Paul said. "For the sake of our son, we have to stay strong." Then kissed Eva lightly on the forehead.

Paul then went to the barn to look for some clues, anything that would help them get Angelo back. The night is approaching fast, and the moon is starting to show her majestic glow. Paul headed back into the house empty-handed. He cannot find anything. The key, is that it? I must figure out where the other ones are.

When he walked through the door, all the children were happy to see him and ran to give him a big hug. Dinner is on the table, and once again the family gathered—everyone, except Angelo. After dinner, Paul went to his bedroom and started transcribing all the notes that he had made from the cave onto a clean sheet of paper. He also wrote down the details of his conversation with Harry the former owner, but he kept his name confidential.

As he went through his notes, Paul began to realize how closely his experiences had matched the man's advice. Maybe something similar had happened to him and he just had not wanted to talk about it. Now as Paul reflected on their conversation, he remembered that the man was almost in tears. Someday I will know the whole truth, just as he told me I would. But I must be strong and above all, I must not give up.

Paul worked on the project until late that night, getting everything ready for the police department in the hope of expediting the case.

Finally, exhausted, he checked on the children and then went to bed. Eva is already asleep, so he tried not to wake her.

The next morning the sunshine woke them up. Another day, another dollar, Paul thought—and another mystery to solve. In this case, though, it is always the same mystery. Every day there were new clues and findings, but nothing significant is found lately. It is just liked a puzzle. I must piece it all up to get the view.

Since the day Angelo disappeared, Paul had kept the hope that one day his son would be found and reunited with the family. He vowed that nothing would make him stop looking until he finds his boy. Until that day came, Paul would keep collecting clues and information, every little piece of the puzzle, hoping someday to put them all together to get the picture right. He knew now that his son is alive somewhere, just not with his family. Until that day came, Paul would not quit asking, seeking, and searching.

On the day of Angelo's return, all his tears and effort would be worth it, and his family would be whole again. Until that day, however, Paul had to accept the cruel reality that his son is still missing. Fortunately, the local police departments were all in collaboration with him and had shown the family their full support. The police were supposed to be the one doing the investigation, not me! Paul thought.

CHAPTER 6

The blackbird's Capture.

Paul came up with the idea of setting a trap to lure the blackbird into returning. He bought some birdseed, dug a hole in the dirt, and then buried a cage with an invisible entry. Every day he visited the trap to look for some sign of the bird, but for a long time, he found nothing. Then one morning after breakfast, he visited the place and noticed that there were some fresh tracks on the ground. He looked more closely and saw that they appeared to be a bird's footprints. Here we go, he thought. A couple of more days and I will get this bird. He added more birdseed to the trap. As he walked home, he covered up his own tracks, just in case the bird might see them and never come back. He kept up this routine for a week.

Then, one day he had an encounter with the bird. As he was on his way to the trap, he noticed something. Paul stopped and squatted down. Slowly he lowered himself to the ground where he sat and looked in the direction of the movement. Sure enough, the blackbird is there. Paul could see it clearly, but the bird did not see him. I will get you, dear bird, and I will keep you hostage until you tell me where my son is.

Paul waited for the bird to take off, and then carefully he stood up making sure that the bird is not around. He strode over to the trap and saw that the bird had eaten some of the seed, but not all of it. He also noticed that it did not come close to the trap; apparently, it sensed something wrong. So, he walked back to the house, grabbed some baking soda, and went back to the trap and added more seeds, covering the ground with baking soda and then with dirt. Again, covering up his tracks, he walked home.

Once inside the house, Paul ran to tell his wife the news. He is quite sure that he had seen the blackbird in question. "Only time will tell if I am right," he said. "I do know one thing; that bird is furious.

You may remember that the blackbird had a band around its leg, just like a pigeon? Well, this one did too, so I feel confident that it's the one." After a good cup of coffee, Paul had to take off for work, leaving Eva to keep a close eye on the area from the house. He called from work a couple of times to ask if she had seen anything unusual, but she said she had not. After work, Paul drove by the store to buy more birdseed. He had almost emptied the entire store's seed when the owner asked him, "Do you feed all of the wild birds in this area?" "No, but the bird I am feeding is a pig," Paul said.

After that, he is on his way home and he is hopeful that maybe soon he would have the bird in captivity to answer some of his questions. But how can I get this bird to talk? He wondered. He did not know anyone trained to make birds talk, but he is planning on holding the blackbird hostage until Angelo is returned to him, safe and sound.

When Paul arrived home, he began the night's routine checking everything—the garage, the barn, and the tractor. After the inspection, he went to the trap to see if the blackbird had eaten the seed. To his surprise, all the seed was gone, but there was still no bird. Well, you smart bird… I will get you, and once I do, you will pay for all the seed I am buying now to capture you. Paul went back to the house and grabbed more seed. After filling the trap and making sure all evidence of his presence was covered, he returned to the house.

He arrived home just as the children were coming back from the lake. "Hi, Dad!" said one of his daughters. "We're happy to see you back!" "Hello, everyone," Paul said.

"I am happy to see all of you guys too. Did you notice anything unusual while you were at the lake?" "No, Dad, nothing special," his daughter said. "Why?"

Paul then explained what is happening, and the children were excited that soon they would be able to give the blackbird a piece of their minds.

"For now, please don't go near the trap," Paul said, "because I have the feeling that I am just about to capture that ugly bird."

"No problem, Dad," one of the boys said. "You can count on us—we want to see it too." At that, Paul was reassured that his children would not foil his attempt to capture the bird.

From that day forward, Paul never gave up on his quest. He spent thousands of dollars trying to catch the elusive fowl. He did not care about the money; all he wanted is the blackbird. Finally, Paul called Harry, the mansion's former owner, to ask him if he had ever seen the bird.

"Of course, I have, many times," the man said. "Every time something bad happened, I would have seen him just a few days before."

"Well, thank you for letting me know about this little detail," Paul said. "I guess I will have to be more careful over the next several days. It has already been two days since I have noticed that the bird is in the area again. Did you ever try to capture it?"

"Yes, I did, but I never had any success. This bird is highly intelligent and doesn't fall for just anything."

"Oh, I know," said Paul. "But it's just about to find out that there are others who can outsmart him."

"I just knew from the day I met you that you were the right person to get to the bottom of this. Do you remember when I told you that?"

"Yes, I do, but I—I was not sure if I trusted or believed you." "That's okay," Harry said. "Because now that you understand what's really happening, I am sure that justice will be served."

"On that, you have my word," Paul replied. "Let me tell you, there is not a day that goes by without me thinking about the bird."

"May I ask why? I don't want to be nosy, but...,"

Paul is surprised that Harry did not know about the recent events at the mansion because he had always suspected that Harry knew something. "My son mysteriously disappeared," Paul said. "He disappeared without leaving a single trace, not even his shoes." "Boy," Harry replied. "That must have been hard on you and your family. But

I will tell you one thing; you are not alone. I suspect that everyone who ever lived in the mansion left the place because of something similar, but I don't know for sure."

As much as Paul wanted to know more, he had to get home. "Can we continue this conversation at another time?" Paul asked. "How about if I invite you to my house and we talk about it further?" "I would love to do that, but if you want to have the conversation in person, it is have to be before the end of next week," Harry said. "After that, I am going on vacation for two weeks, and by the time I get back, many things could happen that might have been avoided."

"Okay," Paul said. "I will get back to you in a couple of days, depending on my schedule." He hung up the phone.

This is a significant development in the case, and as Paul walked home, he daydreamed about the safe recovery of his missing son. The night is close; the moon is already replacing the sun in the sky. Paul decided to go home and make sure that all the doors were properly closed and locked.

First, he walked to the lake, entered the tent where the children already had settled into their sleeping bags and told them to be extra careful because he sensed that something big is about to happen. Then, he walked to the trap to make sure that it is full of birdseed and the cage is still well hidden and tied down so that the bird could not take off with it. Then, he headed home.

As he entered, Eva exclaimed, "I have the feeling that we're on to something here. The pieces to the puzzle will soon be as abundant as water in a river."

The following morning, Eva told Paul about a dream she had had. "Well, my dear, I dreamed last night that we caught the blackbird. However, I also dreamed about the consequences of capturing it."

"Never mind the consequences," Paul said. "I just want to capture this creature. The day I do, well, it will be put on trial as a prime suspect in the disappearance of our son Angelo. Can you imagine the police department with a blackbird for a prime suspect? For now, though, I must be patient because I am sure this wise creature has a sense of danger and will not just fall for just anything.

That bird has probably been conditioned to face many kinds of situations—I know messenger birds were considered brilliant. Do you remember the parakeet in London that was apprehended as a prime suspect?" "Yes, I do remember," Eva said. "That may prove our point here, and I just know in my heart that we are onto something." With that, Eva went to the kitchen to fix breakfast for the family while Paul headed to the trap. This time he noticed something different.

Judging from its tracks, the bird seemed to have come close to the door of the cage, but for some reason, it left. Paul decided to examine the cage to see if he could find out why. He looked closely and discovered that a tiny corner of the door had been left uncovered. Well, Paul thought furiously. I almost got that blackbird. Smart creature—you will not get a second chance, believe me.

The children, who were making their way home from the lake on a gorgeous morning, were more cheerful. They arrived at the house just in time for breakfast, jumped into the shower, and then set out again to go back to the lake. On their way, they stopped by the barn to see their dad.

"Good morning, guys," Paul said. "How was your night?" "Fine," they said, almost in unison. Then, one of them said he had dreamed that the blackbird was captured and brought to justice. Paul was pleased to hear that. Truth comes out of the mouths of children, he thought.

"Well, children," he said after giving them a big hug, "be careful on the way to the lake, and have fun."

"Yes, Dad, we will. Do not worry, we will. Everything will be simply fine." With that, Paul left for work.

Again, that day Paul stopped on his way home from work to buy birdseed, as well as some hard cheese. As soon as he arrived home, Paul is busy setting up the trap, putting the cheese on the very corner of the cage, just past the flap that closed the door. This time I am sure to get the bird, he thought. After setting the trap he covered up anything that could cause the bird to be suspicious, hoping that this time it would finally be apprehended and brought to justice.

The children, as usual, were enjoying themselves at the lake; Eva is busy in the kitchen, and soon dinner is on the table. As the children gathered around to eat, Paul noticed that the atmosphere seemed somehow brighter that night and he had a strange feeling that something good is about to happen. Still, Paul reminded the children to be incredibly careful, and that if he apprehended the blackbird, they should be aware of possible repercussions.

No one knew where the bird came from or who owned it if anyone did. These details were still vague. But what is clear is the fact that their brother had been missing for weeks now, and that this blackbird had something to do with it. The children became serious and promised to be extra careful. They realized that Paul is growing more and more reluctant to let them go to the lake for the night. They were afraid that one day, their father would refuse them this privilege altogether, and so they were careful to respond to his fears and reassure him.

As Paul jumped into bed that night, He said to Eva, "You know dear, I have this strange feeling again." Then they both fell asleep.

Around midnight a sharp squawking woke up the whole family. Paul jumped out of bed, exclaiming, "It's the bird!" Eva also woke up to investigate the funny noise. As for the children, they were too scared to move, rolled up in their sleeping bags by the lake. Flashlights in hand, Paul and Eva hurried to the site of the cage. Sure enough, there it was the blackbird, furious. "There you are, you ugly thing," Paul said. "I have been feeding you for a long time. I am sure you remember me now." The blackbird threw itself against the cage, not letting Paul and Eva near, so they just made sure that the cage is well secured and returned home for the rest of the night. After a while, the creature settled down and things returned to normal again.

The next morning, the children were up early and still scared from the night before. The loud screeching had alarmed them, so they were awake but afraid to step out of their tent. Paul is worried; the children usually were up and running around by now, but they were nowhere to be found. He hurried to the lake, opened the tent, and found the children inside, pale and trembling. "What's the matter with you guys this morning?" he asked.

"Didn't you hear that loud noise last night?" Ron replied. "It's so scary that we all bundled up together. We were afraid the bad guy was on his way to the lake."

THE BLACKBIRD'S CAPTURE.

"Oh no," Paul said. "The noise came from the blackbird. I have finally captured it."

The children were overly excited about the news. "Oh, Dad, can we go see it?" one asked.

"Yes, you may go, but I want to be there with you," Paul said. "Last night the blackbird is so furious he would not let me anywhere near the cage."

Soon they had gathered near the cage, where the bird is letting out shrill screams that terrified everyone. Paul leaned toward the cage and said, "Now, blackbird, I finally got you and you better start talking."

Paul and the children walked together to the house, where they found Eva worried because it had been almost an hour since Paul left to check on the children. "My goodness, I am happy to see you guys. If you had been any later getting home, I would have had a nervous breakdown."

Paul replied, "My dear, the children were scared by the noise last night—I found them frozen with fear in their sleeping bags."

That morning, the family enjoyed a profound sense of relief and happiness; it is like the beginning of a new era in their home. As usual, the children took their showers, and they were ready to go back to the lake. At the door, they asked for permission to look at the blackbird on the way. Paul replied, "No, and don't go there without me or your mother." They promised not to and took off for the lake.

Now that Paul had captured the blackbird, he is cherishing every minute of his victory. "I'll teach you to attack me and my son. You won't have long to wait to see your fate."

He called the police department to report the great news, which pleased them. Paul proposed that they call a veterinarian for help because the blackbird is obviously in a rage and would not let anyone close to it. "I think we'll have to put it to sleep before we try to get it out of its cage," he said.

The police agreed and called a veterinarian to see if it is possible for him to put the blackbird to sleep so they could safely transfer it from the cage on Paul's property to a secure room at the police station. "Not a problem," the veterinarian said. "I will be there in fifteen minutes."

65

Meanwhile, the police arrived at Paul's property and were able to see the blackbird in the cage. Shortly afterward the vet arrived. The vet pulled on heavy gloves and put the bird to sleep with an injection. Carefully the police removed the blackbird from the cage and examined it, noting the number inscribed on a tag on its leg. Then, they asked the vet to follow them to the police station and asked, "How long do we have before the bird wakes up?" "A couple of hours, max," he said.

"Well, we don't have any time to waste here," the lead officer said. The men all entered their cars and drove, lights flashing, back to the police station where a room had been made ready for the bird's interrogation if it could be called that.

While the bird still slept, the police ran what appeared to be a serial number that was on its leg. It provided some interesting information to be analyzed.

It appeared that this blackbird once belonged to a long-dead magician whose own family vanished without a trace not long after his own death. This information took the investigation to a totally new level. Now the police had something to look for.

Paul, after releasing the bird to the police, returned to the house to talk to his wife and children about what had happened. As he arrived, Eva whispered, "What are you hoping to achieve with a bird that can't even talk?"

"What do you mean?" Paul replied. "We already know a secret about the bird."

"What secret is that? Do you know where our son is?"

"No, not yet" Paul said, "but we know some personal information about the bird. We know that it had a master, a magician who died a long, long time ago, and that the rest of the magician's family vanished without a trace not too long after his death."

"Oh, that sounds interesting!" Eva said. "And how is that even related to Angelo?" Eva is getting impatient. "The sooner you find our son, the better for me I want out of here—bad."

Paul called his work to tell them an emergency had come up and he could not make it in. They understood and gave him an extra day off to take care of things. In the meantime, the children were once

The Blackbird's Capture.

again spending their days at their favorite place, the lake. Now that the blackbird had been apprehended, they were more relaxed and content.

After a couple of hours in its room at the police station, the blackbird started to awaken letting out such a loud squawk that the entire police station was taken by surprise. It also started to fly at the walls, trying to get out, but there were no windows through which it could escape. The vet is standing by to examine its condition.

While this is going on, Paul was at home, sipping a cup of coffee with his wife. One thing had occurred to Paul: the fact that the mansion's former owner Harry had left for two weeks of vacation the very day Paul captured the blackbird. What a coincidence, he thought. Or maybe I am just overreacting.

So, the blackbird belonged to a magician who might have put a curse on it. This changed the whole scenario. What had happened to the bird before it entered the lives of Paul and his family? Had it ever been used to commit a crime? If so, this would explain a lot, but clues were still missing. Sure, having the blackbird in a secure cage would probably be better since they have it under control. Now, Paul does not have to worry about being pecked and pooped on again. He is jubilant. Happy he finally got the blackbird.

"Time and patience," Paul said to himself. These where the same words Harry had used—but why the need for such time and patience? How long had this situation been going on? How many families had fallen victim to the tragedy at the mansion and simply walked away from the place? Curious, Paul went to the local library to see if he could find anything, any history or testimony about the mansion. He searched the address and discovered that at least three families had experienced similar fates. Who were these three other families, and where are they now? Maybe if they had stayed on course and not given up, they would have had the courage to come forward with their histories and with all the pain and suffering. For the time being, Paul had to focus on his own family because the more time went by; the less likely it is for Angelo to be found.

After the blackbird's capture, Paul had given the police all the details of his investigation of the cave including its height and precise entry point. He dreamed of going back there when he had more time to explore. He knows that it is extremely easy to get lost forever in a cave like that. Even with the marks he had made on the walls, there is no guarantee that he would not get lost if he went back in. Anyway, the important fact is that he had found the cave at all and taken it upon himself to explore it.

Paul thought about the fight he had with the blackbird on his way out of the cave, and he also remembered the last conversation he had had with Harry, who had urged him to look for the cave. Clearly, Paul thought, this cave had something to do with the disappearance of my son. Then there is the fact that the cave is apparently maintained by someone or something; everything is unusually clean. True, it was not orderly like a home, but without a doubt, there is some activity taking place there. It is likely, therefore, that the blackbird is not the only perpetrator.

In the meantime, the police were taking the case seriously because, for the first time ever, the case related to the mansion had progressed. They were encouraged by the fact that now they got clues and notes and a black bird for interrogation, at least they have something! As they searched for more clues, they ran background checks on some other people in the area to see if anyone around might have something to do with the blackbird, but no immediate results were found. Paul, on the other hand, knew something about the case that the police did not have knowledge about and it involved the former owner.

One thing Paul could not resolve is why Harry knew so many details of the situation since he claimed not to have anything to do with it. Paul found it odd, but he decided not to talk about it for now because Harry could be helpful in finding his son. Right now, Paul's focus is to ensure his own safety and that of his children. Ultimately, Paul's wife and children were the only things that mattered, and nothing could change that. Now with the blackbird in captivity, his focus is to find his lost son no matter what it took. He just wanted Angelo back where he belonged. He desperately wanted to go back to the cave.

CHAPTER 7

The Meeting

With the blackbird in captivity, the police arranged a time to go back to the cave with Paul. Investigators would be there to fully inspect the cave. Paul liked the plan, so he coordinated a time when Eva would be able to stay with the children. As for them, Paul had everything under control; he would ask his children to clean the upstairs of the barn. Paul spent many hours looking for clues there, but he never found any except for the little key that he had noticed the first day.

The upstairs of the barn is filled with boxes of toys and all kinds of things left from previous homeowners. This is one thing that the children had always wanted to do – cleaning the barn but with Angelo gone, they do not feel the need to do it anymore, it is his idea in the first place. So, everything is now arranged, and the barn looks cozy. Meanwhile, the police had written down the number found on the bird's leg and given it to the investigators.

While all of this was taking place, Harry was back from vacation and dropped by to see Paul, who was relieved to have him in the picture again because he had more questions to ask Harry and was dying for answers. He invited Harry in for a cup of coffee. "How's your trip?" he asked.

"Just fine," he replied. "It's been a long time since I had such a peaceful vacation."

"That's good to hear," Paul said. "Now that you are back, may I ask when you have to go back to work?"

Harry seemed a bit surprised. "Why?" he asked. "Remember the previous conversation we had, I asked you to not incriminate me in this whole ordeal?" "Yes, I do," replied Paul. Harry then said, "I swear I had nothing to do with it."

"I am not trying to incriminate you. I was just wondering if you could come with us when we search the cave."

"What do you mean by 'us'? Remember, our deal was that you would keep our communications a secret and not reveal my identity to anyone."

"That's exactly what I did," Paul said. "No worries. But I thought it would be a good idea for you to come with us."

"Let me think about that," Harry said. "I'll get back to you soon." He stood up to be on his way home shortly after the conversation, leaving Paul with a lot of questions and very few answers.

Once again mysteries his mind was racing, and it drained his energy. How could he let this happen to his family? After his brief talk with his neighbor, Paul realized that he was walking a fine line—Harry had really meant it when he had asked for anonymity. This was a normal procedure in any situation where the details of crimes and criminals had not yet been formally sorted out. Paul knew since day one that his neighbor was very susceptible to mischaracterization, but Harry had never clearly expressed his concerns about it except the day when he mentioned the cave.

As Paul was going to the barn, the mailman pulled into the driveway with two certified letters for him. Paul walked up to the mail truck and the two men exchanged brief pleasantries. The mailman asked Paul if he liked living in the mansion. "Of course," Paul said. "This is a gorgeous place—it's my dream house."

"Do you have any regrets about having moved here?" Nervously, Paul replied, "I don't have any regrets. Why do you ask?" The mailman explained that he had delivered mail to the home for years, and all the previous owners had told him that they regretted having moved there.

"How long have you delivered to this address?" Paul asked. "At least twenty years."

"Then you must know about some of the activity that's gone on in this place." "No, not really," the mailman said. "All I know is that every family that passed through here told me that they lost a son."

Paul was visibly shaken to hear this again from another source. "Did I say something to offend you?" asked the mailman. "No," Paul said. "It's nothing—you just touched on a sensitive subject."

"I am sorry. I didn't intend to hurt you in any way."

"Tell me something—when was the last time you knew for sure that a family lived here?"

"To tell you the truth," the mailman said, "I must have seen this place for sale at least forty times."

"Why wasn't the home's sales history made clear to buyers in the real estate market?"

"I haven't got a clue. One thing's for sure, the former owner really had my attention when he was the owner of the mansion."

Paul's hearted jumped. "What?" he exclaimed. "Are you talking about the man who comes here all the time?"

"Yes, I am talking about Harry the former owner that I have seen here talking to you from time to time. I do not know. I just have a strange feeling about him."

Paul was more confused than ever, but he tried to collect his thoughts and stay calm. "What's so strange about the guy?" he asked. "Well, for one," replied the mailman, "he believes in extraterrestrial phenomena. I have witnessed it myself at times when he has erected a temple or sanctuary for them. Also, some of his followers gather twice a year in the barn for what appears to be some rituals."

Paul looked at the ground, thinking. "This is unbelievable. Did he have any family?"

"Not that I ever knew of. I remember a couple of times when the yard was full of cars and festivities."

Now that Paul realized that he had such limited knowledge of his strange neighbor, he wanted more information from the mailman.

"Can you give me the specific times and if it appeared to be a certain occasion?"

The mailman thought for a moment and then answered, "Yes, sir—it concerned a blackbird flying around the neighborhood."

The mailman checked his watch and said, "Well, I am ahead of schedule, so sure." He parked his truck and walked with Paul to the house, surprising Eva, who did not know what to make about this strange, sudden friendship. She poured two cups of coffee for the men and then sat down as Paul resumed the conversation.

"Can you tell me if the former owner has something to do with all of the weird things happening here?"

"Honestly, no. But a couple of times I had to deliver some strange mail here—a bad odor was coming out of the envelope. Also, a couple of times, I had a flat tire for no reason on my way back from delivering the mail here."

There are too many similarities here, Paul thought. My goodness, this guy knows something!

The mailman added, "I know that the last family that lived here just before you, told me that one of their sons vanished without a trace. I had a hard time believing it and even told the police that I thought it was suspicious."

"What do you mean by that? Do you think they had something to do with the disappearance of their own boy?"

"I don't know," the mailman said. "All I know is that everything has a motive." The mailman was quiet for a moment and then added, "They seemed to be a very happy family, but I didn't know anything about them beyond appearances."

By now, Paul was about to scream from frustration, but he kept his cool and asked the mailman if he had noticed anything strange going on in the barn. "Of course, I did here and there from the gravel road. I saw some activity, like candle vigils and what looked like rituals."

Paul jumped out of his chair and exclaimed, "So you saw some activity involving the former owner I have been talking to also?"

"No," replied the mailman. "Harry the former owner was at his house at the time. I believe that he did not have anything to do with it."

Reassured, Paul asked, "Do you have any idea where those other people could be now?"

The Meeting

"No, sir, I don't have any idea," the mailman said. "But one thing is for sure, strange things came out of that barn. I believe this barn has much to do with the many misfortunes of the families who lived here. If I were you, I would burn it to the ground to destroy whatever may be the cause of the problems." At this point, the mailman stood up and said, "I am sorry, but I have to go now. I hope I answered all your questions. If you have more questions for me, could we arrange another time to meet? Here is my telephone number. Call me any time you need something." With that, the mailman got into his truck and went back to work.

Paul now knew a little more about Harry and he was prepared to confront him with new questions. Paul opened the certified letters and read them. They were the notes from his brother's and sister's cars. Paul made a photocopy of them both and put the original notes in an envelope addressed to the police department. As he was sealing the envelope, he heard a car pulling in the driveway. Paul looked out the window it was Harry. He seemed agitated, so Paul walked out to his car. "What's up with you today?" Paul said. "What can I do for you?"

Harry did not answer right away; he looked like he was organizing his thoughts before he spoke. "Well," he finally said, "I saw that you had the mailman in your house, and I just wanted to ask you if he talked about me. You know that he and I don't get along."

"I didn't realize that there was a conflict between you two," Paul said. "He just came to talk about some observations that he's made over the years. You know, after twenty years delivering mail to the same place every day, he must have noticed many little details." "Well, that doesn't mean that everything he says is the truth," Harry said. "Whatever he may have seen was from the street."

After acknowledging that there was some truth to what Harry was saying, Paul pressed on. "Just tell me if it's true that some kind of ritual happened in the barn." "No," Harry said. "No, there were no rituals in the barn—just children who slept in it, only to disappear without a trace." Paul jumped from his chair and exclaimed, "What did you say?" "You heard me, and yes, some children did vanish," Harry said. "Do you know how these children disappeared?"

"Not at all," Harry said. "That's why I decided to do some research about the situation and the possible causes." "Did you come to some conclusion? Did you discover anything? Any trace?"

"Yes, I did, except for some small details; I couldn't find anything to shed light on the mystery." Harry reached over to the seat beside him, picked up a notebook, and presented it to Paul. "Here is my own little investigation," he said.

Paul was pleased to receive the notebook and was dying to go through it to find more clues to the whereabouts of his son and if possible, the others. "Thank you very much for all your help," he said.

"Don't think I have anything to do with these disappearances," Harry said again. "Honestly, I don't. I am tired of being judged and misjudged by everyone. Let us get one thing straight; if I had something to do with this situation, I wouldn't have given you my own research."

Paul stood there quietly. Then, after a moment, he said, "Well, I understand your concern. But why didn't you give me this before?" "I do have other things to do. And besides, it was somewhere in the house, and I couldn't find it." With that, Harry said good-bye and backed out of the driveway.

Soon Paul was pouring through the pages of Harry's notebook. He found a few new clues—nothing overly exciting, but they reinforced the idea that Harry was being truthful. He finished reading the notebook, copied down a couple of interesting passages, and then put it aside to work on something else for a change. Just then the phone rang. It was Ron, his brother, asking if he had received the certified letter. "Yes, bro," Paul replied. "I just received it, and now.

I am getting ready to go to work." "Do you have a second to talk?" "Of course, I do."

"On our way home, I was thinking about the fact that Angelo wasn't there at your housewarming party." Paul's heart beat a little faster. "Of course," he said. "I sent him to stay with one of his uncles who couldn't come up last Saturday." "Fair enough," his brother replied. "Just wanted to ask, because. I know how much you love your children."

"Thanks for asking," Paul said. "And how's your family doing?" "My family is doing fine. And we'll be back in a couple of months—my boys really enjoyed the beautiful lake." "You're welcome any time," Paul said. "Just let me know ahead of time."

Ron also mentioned the cave—how exciting an adventure it had been for the children, and how they had talked for days about the experience. "I am glad they had as much fun as I did," Paul said. "You know, I think the place has a mysterious appeal."

"I do too. Since we have been home, not a day goes by without the children talking about it. Something powerful is in there. My children usually are not very adventurous, that cave seemed to bring out another side to their personalities."

Paul was happy to hear that his nephews and nieces were acquiring a taste for the outdoors. He began to wonder exactly what gave the cave that mysterious, magic touch. After reflecting a while, he concluded that this appeal might have been the cause of Angelo's disappearance, and possibly other children's also. Paul called the police to report that he had some new information for them.

"How long would it take for you to get here?" the investigator asked. "I can be there in a couple of hours—just enough time to put things away and get things under control here at home." "Don't rush, we've made some interesting discoveries?" the investigator said. "Right now, we are studying them to see if there is any relationship between the ants and the disappearance of your son Angelo."

"So, you have come up with new clues?" Paul asked hopefully. "Yes, we have, right now we have to get back to work. See you in a couple of hours." Paul is in the kitchen, relaxing and drinking a cup of coffee, when Eva walked in, saying, "You sure are in a pleasant mood today. You must have some good news." "Yes, I do, my dear," Paul replied.

"Well, I hope you're in the right path," she said. "I miss him dearly" "Trust me, dear," Paul said, "just trust me. Oh, one thing before I take off, I would like the children to clean up the upstairs of the barn sometime today. Would you be willing to be there with them?" Eva answered, "Absolutely."

Paul gave her some specific instructions and was planning to drop by the police station. Eva now knew that one of the clues may be in the barn, and she is ready to tear that barn apart until she found it. Paul arrived at the police station less than two hours after his initial call. He presented the evidence that he had collected, as well as the certified letters from his brother and sister. With that evidence in hand, the investigators were able to add their own finding that led them to come up with more answers than Paul had by himself. This whole situation has too many coincidences and clues to not be resolved soon, Paul thought.

Paul asked the investigator what he had found out; he is curious about any new findings. The investigator told Paul that they had run a computer check on the number found on the bird's leg. The blackbird lived in the cave for many years; he had hidden there because he was disliked by people in the area. Evidence showed that the magician likely died in the cave nearly a century ago, although his body was never found. Investigators said his family had disappeared, around the same time as the magician's death, and could not be traced. As the investigator spoke, Paul is trying to connect these new facts to details from the conversations he had had with Harry and the mailman. These sources were essentially saying the same thing.

The investigator told Paul that the police department is gathering the tools and other materials they would need to explore the cave. Paul told the police that his children were spending the day cleaning the upstairs of the barn, where previous homeowners had left a big mess. "You know, I just don't have time to clean up everything myself, and my children have wanted to do this for quite some time. I have asked my wife, Eva, to supervise them.

There is no question of them going in the barn by themselves," Paul said. The investigator commended Paul for his good sense, adding, "Make sure that they collect anything interesting that may help the case move forward." The policeman than suggested that Paul invest in guard dog for his property. Paul agreed, saying he would buy a dog on his way home, at the animal shelter.

Paul had thought about getting a dog before, but he had never done it because he assumed that the rest of the family would not care about it. They had always lived in a big city and never had need of a dog. But now they were living in the country, and the children were starting to get used to rural life.

The Meeting

Paul went to the animal shelter and asked for a dog that had some training and an instinct to guard. The shelter's manager said, "I believe we have the perfect dog that would fit your needs—it's an older Black Lab." The store owner led Paul to the dog cage; Paul could see that it is a highly intelligent dog. He bought the dog right away. Shortly afterward, he arrived at his house and introduced the newest family member to Eva and the children. The children were thrilled to have a new friend; they walked it and played with it.

As for Paul, he is happy to see that the children were pleased with the dog, which they named Molly. It is full of energy and pep; always ready to run and play. That allowed Paul to enjoy more quiet time and uninterrupted conversations with Eva, who is pleased to hear all the progress of the investigation. Paul and Eva had paid attention to every detail desperate to have their son back. Eva also agreed that it is necessary that she be present in the barn while their children cleaned the upstairs. She certainly did not want to lose another child, and she also wanted to ensure that any evidence found in the barn is carefully preserved.

As Paul and Eva discussed the case, they knew the police department is conducting a final inspection of all the tools they would need for the mission to the cave.

Paul is deep in thought as he walked to the barn to begin searching for any evidence he might have overlooked. After a couple of hours of searching, nothing new had surfaced, so he walked back home. Eva greeted him at the door, saying that while he was out the investigator had phoned and wanted Paul to return his call as soon as possible. Paul immediately picked up the phone.

The investigator wanted to confirm that Paul is still on for the next day's expedition. "Yes, we're on the same page," Paul said. "Do you need anything else?" "No, I don't think so. I think we are ready to go." After Paul hung up the phone, he asked his wife what she thought about inviting Harry along to investigate the cave.

"Well, if you trust the guy that much, why not?" Eva said. "He's been around for a long time, and I am sure he could be a great help." With that, Paul called Harry to ask if he is willing to visit the cave with the police and investigators. "Sure," Harry said, "but you'll have to treat me like an anonymous volunteer. I am afraid that I will get dragged into something that I honestly don't have anything to do with."

Paul promised that he would keep Harry's identity secret and that no one would ever suspect that he is the former owner of the mansion.

CHAPTER 8

The return To the Cave

Saturday morning, equipped with all their technology, the investigators joined the police task force and drove to the mansion, hoping to find more clues and solve the mystery once and for all. Paul was not home; he is on his way to pick up Harry, who for now was simply his "best friend." The two of them arrived not too long after the police and the investigators. Harry is a little surprised to see so many people going to the cave.

Paul offered everyone a cup of coffee and packed lunch for the whole group, and soon they were on their way. It is too early and still quite dark. The group planned to spend the whole day at the cave.

At the foot of the mountain, the group stopped to put on their backpacks and gathered the tools they would need to climb the mountain. Then they followed Paul up through the path in the mountain because he had been there before and mapped the way to the cave. They soon arrived at the Y and the sign for Blackbird Trail. Everyone in the group looked at the sign and had the same reaction as Paul when he first saw it. Even Paul immediately thought of the blackbird flying back and forth, but this time Paul knew it would be nowhere to be found. The group arrived at the entrance of the cave, lit their lanterns, and made their way in. Soon they had a good view of the cave's interior; they could see that the place had been somewhat left clean.

They reached the first big room and walked inside. One of the investigators had brought the number taken from the tag on the bird's leg. Ready to face any eventuality there, they began exploring the walls, the ceiling, and the other features of the space. At first glance, it simply seemed like a vast room, but they were about to find a big surprise and mystery that had occurred a century earlier.

The group decided that everyone would stay together, or if they had to split up, half would go one way and half would go in the opposite direction. They would take no chance of losing anyone—not with all the strange stories coming out of this distinct place. The cave is vast enough to hold three hundred people. Its magnitude, with its well-cut walls, would be a perfect place for hiding from the enemy.

Harry is immensely helpful and seemed excited to be there because he had wanted to explore the cave for so long. He had known about the cave and where it is, but he had never had the courage to go in alone. Now, with the police and investigators by his side, he felt that it is meant to be. He saw immediately that the entrance has no indication of what is inside. At first, it looked like an ordinary cave, nothing special; only as you walked deeper into its secret interior did you realize how big it is.

The investigators' first impression of the cave matched Paul's description of it; only one big room could be seen. Making sure that the number retrieved from the bird is kept handy; the group spent half an hour in the big room. Paul joined Harry, who had discreetly separated from the rest. A bit surprised and amused, Harry remarked, "Well, here we are, my friend—right in the middle of the hundred old mystery trying to figure it out."

Paul asked. "Do you mean that you actually know this area?" Harry smiled. "You know, I have been investigating this for years, I was never as close to solving it as we are today." Paul relaxed, pleased to hear this. Then he asked, "Do you know if there is a hidden door into this cave? I am curious to know."

Harry replied, "If I give you the answer, you'll have to act like you've discovered the secret by yourself. Remember, all I know is what

I found out through my own investigation." "Well," Paul said. "just as we have agreed, you know more, just take the lead and I will follow. No one here suspects anything; everyone just thinks you are my best friend."

Harry looked more relaxed as they walked through the vast room, moving farther away from the rest of the group. Obviously, Paul became anxious when he had heard Harry's response. The other investigators were so busy taking measurements that they were not even aware that Paul and Harry were no longer with them. With a sudden burst of inspiration, Paul said, "What if there is a secret door hidden by a false wall?"

Harry gave a nervous jump. "That is possible. Be careful—you must be careful here. Yes, I believe you will find a hidden entrance if there is one. However, you must remember that we actually are in greater danger here."

Hearing this, Paul took a deep breath, suspicious for a moment that Harry is somehow part of a scam; perhaps Harry had been fooling him all along. He briefly considered revealing the identity of his "best friend," but after a quick thought, he instead devised two game plans. "Well," Paul said calmly, "can you at least tell me if you think we're on the right track here?"

"I believe so," Harry said, frankly. "I see all kinds of strange things on the rock here." Together they looked more closely at the cave wall, where they could make out a series of faint lines. Finally, Paul thought he had come up with a possible clue, some strangely formed letters. Paul traced them with his fingers. "Blackbird only enters here," he read aloud. He looked over at Harry. "I think I am onto something here."

"I think so too," Harry said. "It can't be a coincidence that these letters seemed to form in a place where no one, as far as I know, has ever set foot."

Suddenly, there is a loud noise that made them both jumps. The investigators had used a hammer and chisel to remove a piece of the cave wall to collect as a sample. The investigators were awed by the cave's elaborate structure; they had seen many interesting places over the years, but nothing of that caliber.

While the men explored the cave, Eva is at the barn with the children, working diligently to clean the upstairs. So far, they had found nothing relevant to the case, no clue that might tell them of Angelo's whereabouts—just a couple of antiques and magician's artifacts. They did not pay too much attention to them. Still, Eva is determined to find whatever clue her husband think the barn is hiding. After a couple of hours of cleaning, she and the children decided to go back home for a while. Eva, as usual, is busy in the kitchen preparing dinner for the investigators on the mountain.

Back at the cave, the group had so far found no solid evidence that someone had lived there. Meanwhile, being the first ones to crack open the mystery of the cave, Paul and Harry continued to search it diligently on their own. Suddenly, Paul said to Harry, "Look—I think I see a little path going to the left off of this main room." They both hurried toward the spot at which Paul is pointing. Sure enough, markings on the wall identified it as "Blackbird Entrance." "What a coincidence," Paul murmured. "I may have found the secret entrance." Without wasting a minute, Paul, followed by Harry, rushed back to the rest of the group.

When they arrived, one of the investigators asked, "Where have you been? We noticed that both of you were gone just a couple of minutes ago. Did you discover anything?"

"Yes, we did," Paul replied. "Come follow us." Together, the group walked toward the far-left corner of the cave and reached the place marked "Blackbird Entrance." They followed the narrow path cautiously, looking for evidence of a hidden door. On the rock walls along the path, there is a series of letters, which the men wrote down as they passed them. Finally, like puzzle pieces coming together, the letters formed words: you are about to enter the magician realm please make sure he is not sleeping.

The police grabbed their pistols, ready for anything or anyone that would attack them. "Give me my son back!" Paul demanded loudly. "Don't yell!" one of the investigators said. "You're putting us all in danger. You don't know if this magician has an army or special protection." "I am sorry," Paul said. "I lost my cool."

Just then a familiar sight appeared; it is the big rat, which Paul recognized immediately. "Where did you come from, you monster?" he said. When the police asked Paul to explain, he replied, "The first night we slept in the mansion, this rat was in the room where my two girls were sleeping."

As Paul answered, the rat disappeared into the darkness of the cave, trailed by some of the investigators. They decided that it had escaped into a hidden entrance, so they called the others, and the group began knocking on the rock, searching for an opening. They soon discovered that certain areas of the rock sounded hollow, indicating that an interior cave could be behind it. There had to be a hidden door somewhere. Paul and Harry were working together to find it. At one-point Paul whispered, "I wish I had brought my dog with me..."

Then two men announced that they had found the secret entrance; it opened to a stairway ascending to what looked like a vault. Shining their lights down the stairway, the men confirmed that there is a door there and that secret code is required to open the vault. The investigator tried several things to get it to open, nothing worked. So, the group spent a couple of hours in the small room trying everything they could think of to figure out the secret code.

The men had brought some tools with them and were about to use them to pry the door open when Harry said to Paul, "You know I believe that the number on the bird's leg might be the code." Paul immediately walked to the door and carefully began entering the numbers into the lock. He heard it click in response and felt his heart begin to beat faster. What would he find behind this door? What would this vault bring them?

The door popped open, and there, lying at the bottom of the otherwise empty vault is a piece of paper. Nervously Paul reached for it and presented it to the investigator.

It is a map of the secret area in the cave, including the location of the hidden entrance. When they realized what they held in their hands, everyone cheered up and began walking toward the place where the map indicated the entrance.

Paul felt encouraged; he knew they were close to answering all hanging question he had regarding the mansion, his son, and the blackbird. As they approached the place where the hidden entrance is supposed to be, they saw other letters forming on the wall. Again, they took note of these letters and put them together until they had a new message: you are just about to enter the master's realm ask for the servant to open the door.

After he read this, Paul's heart is pumping hard and he is overwhelmed at the thought that he could be rescuing his son. But who was "the servant?" Could it be the blackbird, or maybe the rat? Questions, questions, nothing but questions, the blackbird is far away in a cage, and the rat is not here.

Again, Paul produced the number found on the bird. Harry looked for and discovered another secret entrance and a gate while the rest of the group stood guard in case some army came to the defense of the "master king."

As they had hoped, the number opened the hidden gate, and a whole new place appeared before their eyes. The place is eerily calm and quiet, and the men were surprised to see that the neat space is illuminated by candlelight. The same thought occurred to everyone; either the master is still there, or some servant oversees keeping this hidden palace clean and functional. The silence is deafening; nothing seemed to be alive there. Still stunned that the candles were lit, the group peered around the interior of the spacious cavern. Then, one by one, they walked into the first big room, hoping to find out something or someone.

As they were looking around, the enormous rat reappeared, obviously alarmed that intruders had entered. Immediately Paul exclaimed, "There's the rat! Until now I sort of doubted that he's part of this." He tried to catch the rat but was not fast enough; it disappeared into yet another secret door. The group followed it, not suspecting that they were about to become prisoners of the cave.

Once again, Paul used the number as a code to open the little door, and they all walked through it. But before anyone thought to prop it open, the door closed behind them. Harry tried to open it, without success. The men then realized that they were prisoners of the master of the cave. Paul tried to stay calm. "Let's use our time here to thoroughly investigate this," he said. "Let's see if we can find another clue, perhaps a number, lying around somewhere."

As they investigated, they soon realized that the cave palace had several levels; all the floors were about the same size and were divided by entries requiring codes. They also realized that the lowest level is shaped differently than the others and was more sophisticated. "That must be where the king of this cave resides," said one investigator. The other members of the group were quiet; they just wanted to return home to their families.

Back at the house, Eva had started to become anxious. The children were wondering why their dad and the group had not come back or even called, and Eva tried as best she could to calm their worries, but nothing's working. Everyone seemed to know that something had gone terribly wrong.

The police department was also wondering about the team's long absence. They had a backup plan in case anything went wrong on the mission, so they deployed a second group and gave them a description of the cave and a map showing how to get to it. This group also took with them the number from the blackbird. On their way to the mountain, they stopped to ask Eva if she had heard anything from the group since that morning. "No, I haven't," she said, "strange enough I have a feeling something is wrong. You guys should be careful."

"Well, I am hoping that we will be able to rescue them or at least find out where they are," said the group leader. "It could simply be that they lost their way because the cave is so big. Anyway, we are bringing more equipment, especially batteries, because by now their batteries must be very weak or entirely run down. After all, they have been in the cave since eight o'clock this morning, and now it's well past nine o'clock." With that, the group left the house in a hurry, hoping to reach the mountain before twilight.

When the group arrived at the cave entrance, they pulled out a copy of Paul's instructions and started to explore the interior. To their surprise, the cave is completely illuminated by candles—not a good sign, they thought. Maybe the first group got trapped or there had been an accident. They proceeded carefully with the rescue mission—if that is what it would be—fervently hoping that the mission is just a little elbow grease and they will be done in no time.

They arrived at the Y intersection, where the sign pointed to Blackbird entry. Here, aware of the potential dangers, they cautiously filed onto the narrow path. They were incredibly surprised at how tidy it was—more evidence, they thought, that someone lived here and kept it clean. How could the police not know this? As they walked deeper into the heart of the cave, they were careful to follow Paul's directions.

One little detail is not clear to them–while they followed the right path at the Y intersection, they then took a wrong turn that led them directly to a big area lit by candles—the same area the first group had found. It seemed charming, even beautiful, they loved the sound of tranquility, nothing in there, nothing but serene silence but soon they snapped back to reality; they were there to rescue the first group, who had not shown any signs of life since that morning. It is now well past ten-thirty at night, and the rescue team is anxious to get on with their mission and get out of the evident danger the cave holds.

As the group continued their search, they did not realize that all their watches had stopped working at twelve o'clock. Oblivious, they worked into the night looking for the initial group without knowing how long they have been there. They finally stumbled onto another narrow path that guided them to a small, well-hidden door.

"Here we are," said the group leader. "Here we go. This might be where the other group was trapped." There is a lock on the door, and the second group tried a variety of numbers to try to unlock it, but nothing worked until someone came up with the idea of using the number found on the blackbird. Sure enough, the combination is right. The lock popped open, and every member of the second group rushed inside the room, so preoccupied with rescuing the fellow group members that they forgot about the door. When it closed on them, they realized that they were likely in the same position as the first group. And just as the first group had, they assumed that they could use the same number to open the door from the inside, they punched in the code with no success.

For a moment, the group stood frozen. They had been sent to rescue the first group, and now they were trapped too! Perfect! They thought.

The return To the Cave

They could feel movement in the air, but they cannot see anything—and then, inexplicably, the candles were blown out and the room surrendered to complete darkness. The horrified group turned on their flashlights and continued to look for a way out. They stumbled upon something moving—an enormous ant, unlike anything they had ever seen before. In fact, so big that they thought it is some extraterrestrial of some sort.

Pulling on gloves, one of the investigators carefully picked up the creature to examine it. To his great surprise, he saw numbers engraved onto its body, so he set it back on the cave floor and wrote them down in his notebook. Just as he finished, the candles all lit up again, "What the hell!" the investigator gasped. The group look at each other with question marks all over their faces. The ant, however, had disappeared without a trace. "This must be the number to open the door from the inside," the investigator said. Immediately they gathered at the door, watching as the investigator agitatedly punched in the number—but nothing happened. "Could there be another door? One where we can use that code?" a group member said. Before anyone could answer, another person in the group exclaimed, "Guys! Looks at the giant vermin here—it is a monster! It could have a number on its belly too. But how are we going to pick it up?"

They group began walking toward the monster rat but soon lost sight of it. They searched the floor for a footprint, any sign that they could follow, but it had vanished into the thin air leaving no trails behind. The rat is gone! They went back to work searching for a way out. At least the candlelight helped them save their batteries, but who knew how long the candles would stay lit?

Back at the police department, everyone's worry had started to mount, they were puzzled why they have not heard of anything yet from the two groups. They were hoping that this is still rescue and not a recovery mission. Suddenly the blackbird, which had been under constant observation, fell onto the floor as if it were dying. The police called the veterinarian, who came to the station right away and examined the fallen bird. It looked like its gone. Until the vet confirmed it. He shook his head. "It's dead," he said. "It's too late to revive it."

The policemen took the bird in one of the offices, placed it inside a box for disposal. They were not superstitious, as one of them noted, but a dead blackbird is not a good sign. After convening the officers disposed the dead corpse in a raven near the precinct ensuring no wild animals come and devore the suspected black bird. A couple of hours went by after the disposal of the black bird something caught their attention: a big white glob dripping down the glass front door. Surprised and suspicious, they looked around the premises but saw nothing further. Maybe it a neighborhood kid having fun with a paint gun, someone suggested.

The next day, the veterinarian returned to the police department to collect the dead blackbird. It had begun to smell; they told the vet it was placed in one of the unused offices, after a couple of hours they transfer it outside supervised nearby ravine. The vet walked to the ravine but to the surprise of the veterinary the box was wide opened and empty! An empty box, the bird is gone!

He hurried back inside the precinct to tell the police it gone. "Maybe another animal came and ate it," one officer suggested. They tried looking outside to see if they will find trails or a feather perhaps. "I would like to think this will be the end of our dilemma with that bird." As they were walking back to the precinct, they looked up and noticed that a blackbird high above them was following behind. "Oh my God, is that the blackbird—" one of the policemen began, and then he stopped. "Wait, he was dead! My goodness, was he feigning dead yesterday!"

Now, well on its way to the cave, the blackbird flew over Paul's house and left its mark on the porch. Eva, worried by the strange goings-on and the fact that her husband and the police still had not come back from the cave, had just stepped outside. She immediately noticed the droppings, and looking into the sky, she saw the blackbird flying toward the mountain. Quickly, she went into the house, picked up the phone, and called the police to ask if the blackbird had escaped. When the officer answering the phone confirmed her suspicion, she told them that the blackbird is on its way to the cave. "Well," he responded, "I guess all we can do right now is wait until the others come back from the cave."

The Return To the Cave

The officer reassured Eva that the police would not let her down and asked her to be patient. "I appreciate your trying to comfort me," she said, "but I have already lost one of my sons, and I cannot afford to lose my husband now." Then she hung up the phone and rushed upstairs to make sure the rest of her children were in their room.

The investigators and police, meanwhile, were still trapped in the cave. The investigators were exploring every little corner of the space and had made some progress. The cave had five floors. The radio they have brought with them is not working at all. They did remember testing it before leaving. The cellphone is no help as well. All their communication tools for some reason are not working. They are not sure if another team is on their way to save them. As for the blackbird, it is getting closer to its home.

The police department dispatched a helicopter to follow the blackbird, but by the time the helicopter is heading to the cave, the blackbird was again at the post assigned to it sound and safe. The helicopter group decided to pursue their mission anyway, and soon they were flying over the cave. The investigation team in the cave could hear the helicopter, but they have no way of telling the rescue where they are. So rather than being encouraged, they became even more cautious and for a moment, they stood frozen and quiet, but soon they mustered their courage and continued to search for a way out.

By then, the blackbird is flying free, flying into a familiar path, into a familiar trail and well into the cave. It is back home. And sensed that he has company.

The blackbird is duty-bound and must make the escape to make sure her family is safe. Many times, it had come close to being killed, and many times it had faked its own death to protect them. Hoping that one day, someone will rescue them.

Inside the cave, the blackbird made its rounds and found that the big rat and the big ant as well as the little mouse, were all safe. These creatures had a special way of communicating that only they knew and understood. The blackbird reassured the rest of these unfortunates that the day of their deliverance would soon come, that it is only a matter of time now. The blackbird ordered them to go and hide on the fourth floor and to stay there until new orders came. So, the rat, the ant, and the mouse made their way to the fourth floor under the watchful eye of the blackbird, making sure nothing bad happens to them.

These four creatures had become a family regardless of their differences. They would, always, watch each other back. But the blackbird is worried because she cannot see the cat. Where in the world is the feline? It must be here; it must be here! Or else -

The members of both groups could sense something is hovering above the cave walls, but it is impossible to tell what it is. They only have one thing in mind, to get out of the damned place and rescue the first team. They can still hear the helicopter outside the cave, and they cannot tell what time it is. How many hours have they been in the cave? All they know right now is they are exhausted, desperate, and perplexed with the things they have seen in the cave.

Harry and Paul were focused, cautious and on the lookout of each other; neither they nor the other group members were afraid. They were confident that they will find something or someone in the cave. As they were busy trying to find markings and secret doors, Paul suddenly exclaimed, "I have been pecked on the head again! I hope it's not that blackbird—surely he didn't escape from his cage.; I had a feeling it escaped getting back at me." As Paul spoke, Harry stumbled upon something shiny but dirty. Harry picked it up and wiped it on his shirt. It is a mirror.

CHAPTER 9

The Magic Mirror

Paul and Harry soon had the mirror cleaned. It appeared to be incredibly old but well preserved. It is an old wooden mirror with detailed gold engravings on the wood. The patterns were that of a Crocus flower creeping from the handle going up the wood around the glass. They called out to the rest of the group, and together the men looked at the mirror to see if it will show numbers or signs. Most of the investigators were indifferent until something strange started to happen.

On the clear glass, they started to see smoke. The mirror had come to life—a voice is coming from it, loud and clear. Paul and Harry were at first surprised and then amused by the discovery, not really paying attention to it. "Seriously? A talking mirror, like what? I am Snow White or something?" Then the magic mirror started addressing Harry by name. "You know, Harry, I have always kept a sharp eye on you," it said.

Harry is obviously shaken by the words—it is one of the first times Paul had seen him taken by surprise. "Why? I have nothing to do with this and all I wanted is to help." Harry said. The magic mirror then replied, "I know, Harry. But I also know that you know more than anyone in this room." "Actually, I—," Harry admitted. "I have witnessed many strange activities that happened in that mansion. But I never could explain them."

"Harry, Harry," said the magic mirror, "you are just about to solve it. Isn't that the reason you are here? You always wanted to come here." The mirror then addressed Paul, who is already speechless. "Paul, you are a brave man, and I know how much you love your son."

Surprised to hear the mirror call him by his name also, Paul replied, "Then where is my son? Give me back my son." "You have to be patient, Paul," the mirror said. "You have to take control, be cautious, be wise, the cues are scattered in the cave like sheep without a shepherd. Patience."

Paul nodded. "I am curious though," he said. "Do you control the blackbird or is it the other way around?" "I know how much you hate that blackbird, but make sure nothing bad happens to it." Paul scowled at the talking mirror. "The Blackbird is no longer in the custody of law enforcement," the mirror replied. "It escaped and is now here with the rest of the family."

"What are you talking about?" Paul shouted. "What family could this blackbird possibly belong to? The first time I saw it was at the barn. It acted like it was dead." "Yes, and you kicked it outside like it's a piece of trash. But that was not your fault—you don't know her yet."

Paul said, "Can we quit talking and tell me where my son is." "Not quite," replied the magic mirror. "First, let me tell you that you are just about to solve some something that occurred a hundred years ago. So again, be patient, Paul. I will tell you something more, but you must wait until you are destined to accomplish here." Paul, surprised, replied, "I am not sure I trust you."

The mirror then said, "I don't think you have a choice. An even if you do, you will not stop until you got your question answered. After you leave this cave, go back to the barn and pay awfully close attention to where the blackbird once lay."

Mystified, Paul replied, "I didn't I see anything there before?" "The bird is protecting things that are important to it," the mirror said. "It's also covering the most critical clue to solving this." "Well then, let me out of here so I can go to the barn and pick up that piece of information before the wind blows it away!"

The Magic Mirror

"You don't have to worry about it," the mirror said. "It will be there when you will walk into the barn." "But my other children are in the barn looking for clues." "I know that," the mirror said. "That's why the cat is there to hide it, so it did not get destroyed."

"Wait you said the cat? I have never seen a cat there before." "Remember, you are not alone," the mirror said. "Others before you have suffered the same treatment. They have left, but you, for the love of your son, decided to stay."

"First of all, I am not comfortable with the idea talking to mirror, but you are right – love" Paul replied, "and only love has given me the courage and the will to stay put and find my lost son."

"You are an honorable man," said the magic mirror. "That is why you have been picked to unriddle this enigma. Yes, after you step out of this cave, you are a lucky man because of the treasure that you hold in your hand." "I don't want to be lucky all I need is find my lost son."

"You will find your son; it is not going to be easy. But with patience, he will be returned to you safe and sound." "So, you know where my son is!" Paul exclaimed. "Yes," the mirror replied, "I do. But before you get your son back, you must finish this task. You are about to be given full access to the cave, but one thing is required first." "What is it?" Harry asked. The mirror said. "You must promise that you will not break anything or take anything out of the cave. If you do either of these, there will be serious consequences."

Harry looked around at the members of the group, who have gathered around, listening to the mirror. "What do you mean? Who else is in this cave with us?" The magic mirror replied, "There are more of you on the second floor. You must tell them everything before you set foot in the rest of the cave."

By now every man in the group is hanging on the mirror's words. Each man swore to abide by the rules and regulations put forward. The magic mirror then said, "One more thing, do not touch or do any harm to the blackbird. It will be there. It has to be there."

"Okay," Paul said. "I will not hurt or touch that blackbird. "Do any of you have still have the number you took from the blackbird's leg?" the mirror asked. "Yes, the officer has it," Paul replied. "I suppose you want us to give it to you?" "Not necessarily. Hang on to it, it will be of great importance. All of you will be the only ones allowed to set foot in the secret cave and explore all of its contents."

Harry said, "How did you know my name?" "Does it matter Paul?" "Yes," Harry said, "but that doesn't tell me who told you." "The blackbird told me," the mirror said. "It also told me you tried to kill it—and came close to succeeding." "What's so special about this blackbird? It's a menace as far as I am concerned," Harry said. The mirror laughed. "I know you have a lot of questions. You will understand everything very soon."

"But now what are we supposed to do?" said one policeman. "You are given access to the entrance of the cave, regroup and walk straight to the library on the fourth floor. Then and only then will you begin to understand what is at stake here."

While the first group is talking to the magic mirror, the second group did not know anything about what is taking place; they were still preoccupied with finding a way out. Finally, they found and followed a path with a ceiling so low that it is almost impossible for them to stand up straight. The path led to a parlor-like room, where the walls seemed thinner but still were made of solid rock. The group is surprised that candles in the room were lit up and the room is as clean as if it had just been swept. The group had not been there long before they heard the echo of voices. "Shh," one group member said. "We are not alone. Quiet,—everyone listens!" The men fell silent at once, straining to hear the voices, which for a while seemed to cut in and out. There is a deathly silence for a moment, and then, sure enough, the sound of a voice could be heard clearly through the rock wall.

"Hello! Hello!" called members of the second group. "Hello, is anyone there?" Still, they heard voices, so, walking with their ears pressed to the wall, they followed the muffled sounds. They seemed to be getting closer and closer—and then, suddenly, they heard nothing more.

"We may have walked too far," said some of the group members. They returned to listen at their original spot, but still, there is nothing more. "We're hallucinating; We're losing our minds." said one of the officers. Back at the house, Eva could not sleep, and the children were now asking her to let them go to the cave and look for Paul. Eva did

THE MAGIC MIRROR

everything possible to calm them, but now, with tensions mounting, they were having a hard time controlling themselves. Not knowing what else to do, Eva called one of her sisters and finally opened to her, telling her everything that had happened.

Her sister was shocked at the news. "Oh dear," she said. "Let me help you. I will be right over. Give me about two hours." "Be careful," Eva said. "Drive safely. We do not need any more.... just be careful okay?" She hung up the phone and joined the children outside. They want their father back at the house, losing Angelo is enough. Finally, they went back to the barn to see if they can find something to help Paul or Angelo. They did not know what to look for and this made them irritable.

"Maybe we're looking in the wrong place," said one of the boys. "Maybe we should start looking in the garage; I always suspected that there is something in the garage. Mom, please, let us check the garage." "I am tired," said another child. "We've been over and over in this barn, and still nothing. and now it looks like Dad's missing. Mom, do you remember that the bad blackbird attacked Daddy also?"

"Yes, son, I do," Eva said. "In fact, I don't even want to think about it because it's too painful. But what about it—are you saying we are targets too? But why would we be? I just don't understand this nightmare—what my family has to do with it." Just as she finished speaking, her sister came walking into the barn and seeing Eva near tears, rushed toward her. "What's going on?" she asked, alarmed.

Eva replied, "I hope nothing bad has happened. I am overwhelmed by everything that has happened since we have moved to this mansion. Everything happened so fast. Next thing I knew Angelo is gone and I haven't heard from Paul yet."

The children were happy to see their aunt, but after a brief welcome, they decided to step out and continue to look for clues, wherever they might be. Eva, uncomfortable with the thought of her children out all by themselves, followed them, accompanied by her sister, who is now fully aware of what had happened. The children walked behind the barn to check the place where their dad had set up the trap, and remembered the markings on the grass—did a flying saucer landed in their backyard? They also remembered the other mysterious discovery they had made there; the enormous ants that they had seen and shown their dad. They recalled that he had picked up some of them, but they were not sure where those specimens were now, or if there were still ants in the area behind the barn.

The ants are nowhere to be found, but they still checked the area further hoping to find something or someone perhaps. They came up empty-handed and frustrated.

One of the children approached her mother and said, "You know, Mom, we're starting to believe that they're just intended to distract us from the real source of the problem. Look, we've been searching for these so-called clues and numbers, and we haven't found a thing."

The other children nodded, obviously frustrated and angry. Eva could see that they could not take this kind of stress anymore.

"Where is my Dad?" her youngest child said. "Mom, what happened to him? What happened to everybody who went to the cave?" Clearly, the children had had enough of this situation; one or two began asking, almost pleading, to get out of the place—which is, in their view, cursed.

"We will get out of here," Eva promised them. "But first we have to find Dad and the rest of them. Don't worry; I am taking this into my own hands." Reassured, the children returned with Eva to the house. Just as they walked inside, the phone rang; it is a police officer calling to see if they had had any news from Paul or either of the two groups in the cave.

"Not a word," replied Eva. "If you only knew how much distress this situation has caused me and my children. What's our next move?" "I understand your concern and how worried you are," the officer said. "We're worried too. But we are not giving up, because we know that the two groups, we sent there are trained and well prepared for whatever they are facing. Something will have to give, and we expect it to happen very soon." "We can't just wait here?"

"Let me put it this way: we hope that by the end of the day, your husband, his best friend, and others will be on their way home. You will have to tell your children to remain calm. Remember, no news is good news most of the time. We the police at the precinct know that you want things to move faster and we too want the same thing. I am telling you what my next move is, I am going there personally to the rescue."

"We have investigated the whole village and trust me when I tell you that we took all of the time and precautions necessary to make sure that we find the truth. We've already conducted hours of investigation of prisoners and people of interest, but so far we've learned nothing that would pinpoint the root of the problem."

"Well, you sound optimistic," Eva acknowledged, "you are grasping at straws and don't have anything to share with me except to be patient." "Ma'am, this police department has lots of officers with many years of experience. The group that went with your husband are physically fit and well trained." "Thank you for your encouragement," Eva said. "What about my children?" "It may be a good idea for you to stay with relatives for a couple of days. I don't think that mansion is safe for all of you."

Eva agreed with the officer; in fact, she already had such a plan in her mind. She hung up the phone and then talked to her sister to see if it would be possible for them to go to her place. Honestly, people of the police department are staring at the blank wall, their unusual suspect—the blackbird had succeeded in escaping from its cage. At least, that the case seemed to be reaching some conclusion, however vague. It is not the first time they had been dispatched to the mansion, and they wanted to solve the missing people cases once and for all.

The white cat is well on its way back to the cave from the barn without having been noticed by anyone. The cat is in a hurry; it had been gone for several hours; he had the charge to oversees the entry to the cave. Soon the cat was back to its duties and its post.

The first thing it noticed is that someone had cleaned the magic mirror. The white cat wondered what that might mean. Could someone finally has found the code and come to their rescue? The cat had spent years at its post, and most of the time it just slept from lack of activity. Now there seemed to be some activity inside the cave, the cat had to protect itself from being seen or captured. It decided to hide on the fourth floor, in the library. So, the white cat made its way cautiously to the fourth floor and hid under the main desk. It quickly fell asleep, as usual.

In the library, a little mouse was there to meet him. The cat looks at mouse straight in the eye. Its wide blue eyes showed worry. As if the rat understood what the cat is trying to say, its sprinted away and camouflage itself in the pile of white books near the main desk.

The mouse is restless. He wanted to see the intruders and see what they are up to. With this, the little mouse made its way to the parlors. It had sneaked in and was able to see all the police and investigators in both rooms and even listened to some of their conversations. As it made its way back to the library, one of the officers saw it, "A white mouse! Do we need it?"

"Let's get it," an investigator replied. "There could be numbers embedded on it!" The men chased the mouse, but the mouse is too quick. The mouse escaped to the next room and then stealthily moved on towards the library. In the library, the white cat is waiting anxiously. What the white cat wanted to know is whether he needed to intervene. On the fourth floor, the white cat waited, relieved to see the little mouse walk in the door.

The rat seemed so agitated. The cat just stared and released a soundless purr. They heard a loud crack echoing through the cave. Frightened, the white cat swiftly stood up, quietly waiting, it is back arched and its fur standing on end throughout its whole body covering the white mouse making sure no one will hurt his little friend. Then nothing but deafening silence.

They went into hiding; they knew they did not have much time. They also knew from experience that all visitors had to go through the library to get anywhere else in the cave—if they had the chance to do so.

As the cat and the mouse suspected, the loud noise indeed came from the magic mirror, which had announced to the group, "Okay, you have my permission to explore the cave, but remember, do not attempt to take anything from the cave. If you do, there will be severe consequences for the one who breaks the rule." The men all swore to abide by the mirror's rule, now more anxious than ever to search the cave. After all their hours of waiting, searching, and wondering, something is finally happening.

The Magic Mirror

As the group watched, the magic mirror split in half, leaving an opening just big enough for one person at a time to pass through. One by one, after being searched by the magic mirror, the men made their way in. When Paul stepped forward, the mirror told him, "Be careful. Don't attempt to do anything to the bird." Paul then stepped into the mirror—a little scared, but ready for anything. Is he? Harry followed him, as usual. To Harry, the magic mirror said, "And you, I praise your patience and dedication. But be careful—don't do anything you may regret." Harry stepped into the entry and disappeared, only to rejoin the rest of the group. To everyone's surprise, they found themselves with the members of the second group.

Once everybody crossed through the magic mirror, it closed itself and it fell covered with dust, lying just as it was when the men first saw it. The first group is surprised, they never realized that another group had come looking for them. For a little, while the group talked, the second group was told what the mirror had instructed. At the same time, Paul was informed that the blackbird has escaped.

At that point Paul took the lead, demanding that no one would do harm to the blackbird and whatever else is in the cave. The cave itself is well-maintained and clean, almost welcoming: obviously, someone is maintaining it. The investigators wondered, could there be cave dwellers in here that they never knew about? They knew all the people in town, and no one mentioned of new faces lately just Paul's family. But how did he survive? It is one question after another, and all the men were perplexed. Certainly, none of them had ever expected to be in a bizarre situation like this.

Harry is a bit reserved but cooperative, supportive, and dying inside for answers after his conversation with the magic mirror. He wondered, is it his curiosity or his dire need to free himself from the allegations? For a while, he thought it is stupid for him to be here risking his life but on second thought, he loved the idea of finally piecing the puzzle altogether. After all these years...finally! The answers he has been waiting for.

Paul, on the other hand, is thrilled just to be one step closer to finding his son. While now Paul knew that Angelo is not there, all he needed to do is to get this over with and he will find his son.

The investigators and police notice how the cave was divided and set up. They could see the bottom of it and could make out a splendid lower level with an impeccably clean fireplace. This must have been where the master of the cave resided. Did he have servants, maid, chef? When they looked around, it is obvious to them that someone was there recently; otherwise, the place would have been moldy, damp, and dark. Every candle is burning perfectly: there is no wax on the walls or floor. The rooms and floors. Spotless.

The men wanted to split up to search the place, but at Paul's insistence, they stayed together. They decided to start on the fourth floor, the library. "We can't make any mistakes here," he said. Everyone nodded in agreement.

There is a problem: they saw a ladder going up is hanging high on the room's walls, it seems there is no way to reach them. "How do we get them down?" Harry asked. "Do they lower automatically? Another code perhaps?"

Suddenly they heard something. "Wait, listen," Paul said. "A voice—did you hear it?"

And strangely enough, it is a woman's voice. More intrigued than ever, some of the men began to call out: "Where are you? We aren't here to hurt you."

"You are entering the palace of my lord," the voice said. "This is the first time in a century someone has entered here. What have you come here for?" One of the policemen replied, "We're here to get to know you and to come to your rescue if you are in need. Are you okay? Now show us where you are."

"I don't want to scare you if I show myself. Is the magic mirror aware that you have entered this cave?" "Yes," the policeman said. "We all have been warned by the magic mirror to treat everything kindly and not to take anything or else—" "Fine," replied the voice. "I have to verify this information before I let you go any further. I will be right back."

"Make sure you tell your superiors—whoever they are—that we're here with good intentions, we are looking for a missing boy." called another officer. Soon they heard wings flapping above them. Paul exclaimed, "Do you hear that Harry? Are you thinking the same thing? Oh my God, this is getting more interesting!"

Harry replied, "A talking mirror, now a talking bird. Seriously?" "If you get lucky, you will know my real identity soon," the bird said, "just follow the mirrors instructions. There are five divisions in this cave. I was told you are given permission to explore the library. And only Paul and Harry can do it. "Do what?" asked Paul.

Addressing the word intended to Paul the blackbird said, "Paul the best thing you ever did was to listen to Harry. You were reluctant and doubtful. Yet you feel his sincerity. You are a remarkable person." Paul and Harry at this time looked at each other, waiting nervously what the bird would say. The police must not know Harry was one of the former owners; the one suspected of the crimes. "Harry—well, I have known him for a long time, and he never gave up after what he has been through.

"But how did you know this?" asked one of the officers. "Paul was right all along. The bird was spying on them." "Again, for the last time, follow all the instructions." the blackbird repeated. "Otherwise, you'll discover nothing else—all your efforts will be in vain."

"Yes, we were already warned," the officer said. "ironically, we are dealing with our most unusual suspect. Excellent!"

"Believe me, there is too much at stake here, for all of you, for you to ignore my warnings." As it was speaking, one of the investigators is trying to reach a ladder but fell short three inches. The blackbird, seeing this said, "Do not attempt to touch the ladders. They will lower down in due time." The investigators quickly stepped back. "How did you manage to get out?", asked the officer.

"That was not the first time someone came close to capturing me—and always, I have found a way out. I must. I need to." "I know that I have had issues with you lately..." Paul said. The blackbird replied, "Do you remember, Paul, when you kicked me out of the barn the first day you moved?"

"I will never forget that. The next thing I knew, you were flying high up in the sky, like you were mocking me." "That was the best thing you ever could have done to me," the bird said.

"How so?" replied Paul. "Are you saying thank you after I kicked your ass?" The blackbird said. "You kicked me in the stomach, it hurts yes. But still, it had to happen. You released me out of the barn." "Why – I don't..." "If you had not, I wouldn't be here today. So many families didn't even have the courage to walk into the barn." Paul said, "That's flattering. Now—how do we go up?"

"Not yet. We are not done. I am still waiting for confirmation. You will know when the time comes because one ladder will move down." "How long will it take?" asked one officer. "We don't have an eternity here." "Paul, I wanted to return to the barn after you kicked me out because I want to show you something in there." "You could have at least told me?" Paul asked. "Are they related to the disappearance of my son? Do you know where my son is?"

"I don't want to frighten you. And lose the thinnest ray of hope we had. Your son is not here; I do not know where your son is. However, through here you will get your son back."

"I'll take the chances and move away from that mansion as far as possible."

"The ladder is the only way to get to the library," the blackbird said. It paused and cocked its head for a moment and added, "I now have confirmation that you all are cleared to go." Before the men had the time to move heading to the hanging ladders, the bird held up one wing. "One more thing; be careful not to step on any animals, make sure they are safe of harm's way." "We will. Now can we get down to business?" asked one frustrated officer. The police were getting impatient. So did Paul and Harry but they needed the details so bad they are left with no choice but to listen to the black bird's ranting.

"Fine," the blackbird said. "Now Paul, you and only you are designated to touch the magic ring. Yes, there is a magic ring in the library, and no one can touch it except Paul. Is this clear?" They all nodded. Roger one of the lead officer replied everyone would comply with every rule and demand the officer said.

"Now, Paul, you will have the ring in your hand. You must place it on top of your wedding ring as soon as you find it." "I am all ears," Paul said. "Here's another detail. While you are wearing the magic ring, you

The Magic Mirror

will join Harry, and then both of you will walk the aisles of the library. In one of the sections, there will be an important clue waiting for you."

"That sounds like a scene from a horror movie to me," said Harry. "What are you up to? What are you hiding up your sleeve, eh?" "You will see." Then, the blackbird continued, saying, "As you walk down the aisles you will be guided by a mysterious light that will shine out of a book. Only Paul can take the book or touch the book.

If you only knew what is at stake here. If you succeed, I—we will be forever grateful to all of you. Paul, remember, you are the chosen one, take the lead and be wise. You will know how to proceed and solve the problem. I am not alone in this place when you get to the library, watch carefully, pay attention to anything moving there make sure you don't step on them."

Then, with a majestic bow, the blackbird said, "I welcome you into the heart of the biggest riddle of the century. Many have dreamed of seeing this day, but they all passed away as the years went by, leaving the riddle unsolved. Be careful, we are counting on you." The blackbird left its perch and flew three circles around the middle of the cave then pooped at them before landing again and solemnly declaring, "With that, I chased away any bad energies that may have been present and ready to harm any of you."

"Holy cow! Do you really have to do that?" exclaimed an officer wiping the carp out of his hair. Paul is silent. So that is it! He was doing that to get rid of the bad energy. He did that to Angelo and now he is gone. That is convincing. He thought.

Then the blackbird took off again; the men heard a loud tick, tick, tick; and a clock appeared on the wall. The bird again lit on its perch. "You have two hours in the library to finish the task," it said. "If you stay past that time, none of you will come out. Only Paul has the power and knowledge to stop the clock if more time is needed." The blackbird made a graceful swoop all the ways down to the floor, where it conversed with what at first glance appeared to be two raccoons. The investigators laughed, and one of them said, "Boy, we're in a zoo! How many more animals will we have to wait for?"

"Don't be deceived by what you see officer, as you can see, I look like a bird, and I fly like one, but I have been touched by a magical experience." "Then what are you?" one investigator asked. "Obviously, you can communicate, and you understand us well. What are you?" The blackbird responded, "That's for you to find out before it's too late."

The blackbird made a circle over the group and around the cave and then, with its wing, flipped what looked like a switch. A ladder from the library began to move down slowly as the men watched impatiently. The bottom of the ladder reached the group platform, where the blackbird stood, and giving orders. "Please be careful. This is the point of no return. If one of you falls, all of you are doomed, never to return."

The men looked at each other apprehensively, visibly shaken. But they had made it into the cave that far; this is not the time to back down. One by one the men stepped onto the ladder, carefully holding onto the rungs. When Paul stepped on, the blackbird stopped him and said, "Since you are one picked for this task, you will be submitted to an extra test. If you can pass this test, you and the rest will move on. This test is reserved for you, you and you alone will perish if you fail. But if you pass, all of you will go on to do the task. The police will be there to make sure nothing happens to you and Harry and the animals."

Then the ladder started to shake profusely as if the rocks were brawling under the cave. It shook so severely at times that poor Paul had a hard time hanging on. He gripped the rung of the ladder so tightly that his hand felt welded to it. All the while he held in his mind the image of his son Angelo. For Angelo, he thought.

"You're doing well," said the blackbird. "You are almost there." By now the ladder had begun to fold, turning ninety degrees upon it. He is fifty feet above the ground. Paul almost fell. Everyone who had already climbed up the ladder exclaimed, "Don't give up, Paul! You're almost there!" Finally, the rumbling stopped, and Paul stepped off the ladder into the library; he is shaking incessantly. He never thought he would go through something like that in his lifetime.

Then it is Harry's turn to step onto the ladder. He is already shaking like a leaf, terrified at what he had seen. Little did these men know that he is afraid of heights. He knew that he also has a task to do, but he had less responsibility and fewer duties than Paul. He is hoping that his test would be a little easier than that of Paul. Carefully he stepped onto the first rung of the ladder, at which point the blackbird is in control, knowing that Harry is totally submissive to her will. Harry, already pale, began begging the blackbird for mercy.

"Hmm, let's see, Harry," the bird said. "You tried to kill me a dozen times, but you never did succeed. And I realized that you should have known me better."

To that, Harry replied, "Oh, my lord, have mercy. There is no price too high for my safety. You know I tried to help an entire family who disappeared from the mansion—you know that I would have done anything to protect that family and that all these years I have chosen to stay as a neighbor in the hope of rescuing them." "Then why didn't you report their disappearance to the police?" the blackbird asked.

"I was afraid I would become the person of interest. You do not know all the things that have been said about me because of the situation. Rumors about me being the one responsible for all the disappearances has circulated the town. I stayed to clear my name." "That's no justification for your actions toward me, Harry, I know you didn't do anything wrong."

"Well," Harry said, "if you know I didn't do anything wrong, then why put me through this sort of test in front of the police and investigators?" "For two reasons," replied the blackbird. "First, you never backed down from your responsibilities. Second, you are innocent until proven guilty."

Harry, trembling, said, "But you are alive and well now. May I express how sorry I am to have tried to do the right thing at the time, without having known the real story?"

"Hmm," the blackbird said. "I see now that you have been reduced to begging for your own life. I am taking into consideration the fact that you acted with good intention, but that is not enough. You wanted me dead."

Poor Harry wanted to step down from the ladder at this point, but he realized at that moment that he is high up in the air, far away from the platform. "Oh my, I am doomed," he wailed. "are you enjoying this? Remember, blackbird, I did not kill you—and as a result, you are here today, taking vengeance."

The blackbird said, "Who is taking vengeance here? I am not!" The ladder now is shaking. Poor Harry is still begging and gripping the bars hard. With that, one of the officers pointed his handgun at the bird and said, "Let him go or I will shoot your head off." "Go right ahead," the blackbird said. "Your weapon was made unusable when you walked through the magic mirror." Immediately the officer tried to pull the trigger, only to find it immobile, he cannot pull the trigger. For some reason, it is stuck.

"See? I could take all of you as my hostage because of that, but I will not. Put your handgun back where it belongs." Humiliated, the officer obeyed. The blackbird then turned its attention back to Harry, who remained terrified. He could see himself taking a plunge right into the heart of the cave because now he is in the middle of it.

"I guess the mirror didn't know this, this is pure vengeance?" Harry asked. "No," replied the blackbird. "I just want to see how far you will go. As you know, your comments have not always been gentle." "Yes," replied Harry. "I guess payback is my reality now. Paul, I guess you're going to do the task alone."

The blackbird said, "You know I won't do you any harm. I just wanted to test your sincerity. You know, we bird see only from up high, and we hear only the echoed words of humans. Often, we are misjudged and, in some cases, put to death for no apparent reason. Was that the future that had been reserved for me?" "Guilty your honor," Harry said in a trembling voice.

"Be careful of what you say, because in this place you are vulnerable—just as I was when you tried to capture me." "First, I want to point out," Harry said, "I didn't know what, err, who you are, "he added in a low voice, "you did some things too, like pooping on boys who soon after, disappeared without a trace, leaving no traces behind. The disappearances happened after you do that. Tell me, where can I find those children, including Angelo?"

"How can you judge the action of a bird? It is an act of nature. I must tell you; I was warning the child—and the parent. And all I received in return were death threats." "Oh, you can talk for goodness' sake, why didn't you say so?" Harry said. "What about when you attacked Paul? What about that time?" "Well, let's see here," replied the blackbird. "Paul, did you try to catch me in order to harm me?"

Paul thought he had been absolved by the bird, and so for a moment he is scared, some other test would pop up and he would be submitted to more abuse. Paul replied quietly, "Yes, I tried to catch you because I wanted to avenge myself, and my son. However, do you remember that I came out of the cave covered with your poop?"

"And you should count yourself lucky that that's all that happened because I was told to do more, but I restrained myself because I see hope in your eyes." As they spoke, the ladder is moving up very, very slowly. Harry is relieved the shaking had stopped. He is looking forward to getting close enough to the fourth floor to jump from the ladder and be free again.

The blackbird finally freed poor Harry, who joined the rest of the group. Staying together, the group walked through the little path that led to the library. Silence. No one said a word. They figured one wrong comment would mean a ticket to their grave. Paul is distracted, his thoughts are running. What if I fail? At times he seemed disconnected from the group and even appeared lost. At one point, one of the officers asked Paul if he is doing all right. "Yes, I am fine," Paul answered. "I just had this strange feeling again. I had this since we moved to the mansion."

As the group walked closer to the library, they noticed that it is pitch-black, unlike all the other rooms in the cave. They knew that they had only a couple of hours to find the clue that the library held for them. At the entrance of the library, the blackbird reappeared and said, "Now, before you do anything here, you must find the magic ring. Without the magic ring, you are done for."

The police were adamant to see what is inside. Cautious what test the bird might be cooking up for them. The bird swung its right wing and an invisible door opened. As they passed through the door, the blackbird started to time them. Finally, they gathered inside, their eyes trying to adjust with the darkness.

Their eyes straining to see where the magic ring might be. Paul's job is to walk back and forth trying to sense where the ring is hidden.

There were thousands of books and rows and rows of shelves—some covered with dust and spider webs, others clean and orderly. Thinking that the neatness of those shelves might be one of the first clues, the group rapidly searched them but found nothing of real interest. Then they went to the less orderly shelves, but they cannot find it. They had been looking for half an hour when Paul went out of the library to speak to the blackbird.

"Sorry to interrupt your timing," he said, "but I have a question to ask you." "Go ahead," the bird replied. "I am all yours. What's your question?" "Where will I find the magic ring? You know we are not your enemies, but I sense you're hiding something, and I don't know why." "You are on the right track; Paul the magic ring will be found on the third row in the library. Once you have found the ring, I will give you anything you want when you're wearing the magic ring." "Thank you."

"I feel sorry for you and for the temporary loss of your son," said the blackbird. "You are just about to uncover something that people from this town and across the nation have been trying unsuccessfully to solve.

The blackbird insisted that Paul not speak to anyone about their private conversation. While they were talking, the group searching the library is beginning to panic; there had been no sign of the magic ring yet, and already at least half an hour, if not more, had passed. Was it two days or three days since they left the town? Who knows? That blasted bird might have been the reason why their phones and watches are not working.

"You must go back to the library before they all go crazy," the blackbird told Paul. "Here is one specific clue for you, Paul; you alone will find the magic ring—and don't forget that. You will have to go by yourself for now to the third ray of the library, and the ring should be shining in the dark."

Paul is now convinced now that he is talking to a person, not to a bird, he did not know who it is. Bu the mirror earlier referred to the bird as she. Who can she be? Nervously, he went back into the library.

"Where were you?" one of the policemen asked angrily. "We didn't see you searching the library. Remember, Paul, we're all depending on you."

"I know," Paul said. "I got this, and I will have my son's back also. I have the feeling that we will not find Angelo here. Instead, I think something else—but I cannot figure what. We only have an hour left to find it."

Calmer now, the group went back to their search. As for Paul, he knew exactly where to go and began walking to the third ray of the library, where the blackbird had told him to go. It is dark here, Paul thought as he neared the space. That must be so I can more easily see the magic ring shining. As he is crossing the third section of shelves, a light caught his attention. Paul rushed to the spot and, there is the magic ring, tucked behind an extremely old book. He had found what he is looking for! But when he tried to move the book, he discovered that it is stuck there, as if it had been glued onto the shelves. Feverishly, he began trying to work it free to retrieve the ring.

Time was going by quickly. As Paul struggled with the book, the blackbird flew into the dark library and said, "As of now, you have half an hour left."

"Thanks for reminding us," snapped a frustrated investigator. "It really looks like you don't want us to succeed. We are already under stress—you don't need to add more fuel to the fire for your own pleasure, blackbird."

Finally, Paul pried the book free and reached the magic ring, carefully blowing the dust off it. Now it really shined. Putting it on top of his wedding ring, Paul said solemnly, "Okay, now I am wearing the magic ring. My first wish is for some light." With that, the library suddenly lit up, and now the whole group could see without stumbling. "My second wish is that our time to be extended indefinitely until we find all of the clues and materials necessary to solve the secrets of this cave."

The blackbird appeared immediately, saying, "Paul, you may have your wish. Remember, no one must attempt to steal any object from this library. Now that you have more time and are not under great stress, I will also remind you not to step on anything that moves.

In the meantime, you are on your own—no more hints from me. I need to attend to something." The bird waited a moment for Paul to take in its words, and then it said, "I owe you one more wish before I disappear."

Paul responded, "Well, blackbird, could I have a talk with my wife and children?" "Sure," said the blackbird. "You may pay your family a visit. I will connect you to your wife and children. They will be able to see you, and you will be able to see them. I, however, must disappear. I will be here, but you will not be able to see me anymore. Everything is in your own hands now." Pop! And with those words, the blackbird vanished from sight.

In an instant, Paul is in the mansion – with his family. Eva saw how Paul suddenly appeared from nowhere. Paul then communicated with his family for the first time since he had left the mansion. Eva is happy to see and hear from him; she had almost given up hope. The children were terribly excited to hear their father's voice. His family peppered him with questions.

"How are you doing? How is this possible? We all missed you. Did you find anything? The police department has been searching for you outside the cave—they are worried because two teams went missing with no word. They will be so happy to know we heard from you. Are you hungry? When are you coming back home? Nothing has changed around here. We looked all over the barn but didn't find anything."

It is one question after another until Paul held up a hand to quiet them. "Listen," he said, "I don't have a whole lot of time here. I have had to get back to work. As for the barn, I would prefer that you not go in there anymore. I will tell you more when I get back." Briefly, Paul explained to his family that the blackbird knew his name and had shown up in the cave. "I will tell you more about it at later," he said. "But for now, I have to keep working in the cave. Do not worry—everyone is okay. Please do me a favor. Call the police department to let them know that we are onto something now and that we are all fine. Also, ask them to stop their activity outside the cave. Trust me, everything is going far better than we'd first expected."

Eva noticed that Paul did not sound anxious at all, but very calm and pleasant. She is surprised yet comforted by that fact. At least Paul is out of danger, she thought, and maybe he had found information to the whereabouts of their son. "Do you have any idea where Angelo went? Is there some sort of ransom to be paid?"

"Eva, I don't think Angelo is in the cave. But there are things there that I have yet to find, and I hope that will tell me where he is." "Well, that's good news," she said. "When do you think you will be finished?" "I am not sure, clocks are not working there, although it may be extremely late. I see its noon. If things keep moving the way they are now, it will be late tonight."

"Good luck, Paul," Eva said. "We can't wait to have you home again." "Same here," he said. "And make sure you contact the police department to let them know we are fine." With that, the connection is broken, and Paul and his family vanished from each other's sight.

Eva is now more at ease, and the children were reassured. She picked up the phone and called the police department right away. At the police department, everyone is worried about the rescue mission. When the phone rang, an officer picked it up immediately. "This is the police department. How may I help you?"

"Hello, there—it's Eva, at the mansion. I have had some fresh news for you." "Oh hi, there," replied the officer. "You sound really good, far better than you have been." "That's because I talked to my husband. I cannot explain it, but we were able to communicate although he is still in the cave. It is almost as if he were here. We had a good talk." "Interesting. Are you sure you weren't hallucinating?"

"No, I was not hallucinating," Eva said raising her voice, "although I had to pinch myself a couple of times to make sure it was real. My children also had to pinch their dad to reassure themselves that he was not a ghost. He told me to let you know that everything is going fine and on schedule, that there is no reason to worry. Also, he wanted me to ask you to stop all activity outside the cave. I told him you were still searching the area."

The officer paused for a moment, and Eva could tell he is skeptical. "How do we know that what you are telling us is true?" he asked. "You want more proof? Ask all my children. They saw and talked to him also."

She could hear the officer take a deep breath. "Okay," he finally said. "We will call off all search and rescue outside the cave. That will save us money and time." The officer immediately took the microphone ordered all search helicopters and ground group back to their posts.

Eva and her children, now hopeful and at ease, were feeling a lot better now. With his promise to come home late that evening, they began working to clean the house and get ready to welcome him. After they finished cleaning, the children asked their mother if it would be okay now to walk to the lake. "Okay," Eva said, "but you have to stick together."

Soon the children were well on their way to the lake, enjoying their liberty. It is the first time they had been allowed to go there since their dad left.

Back at the cave, Paul is busy looking for clues. Now that there is no time limit, they had plenty of time to search the library thoroughly and collect all the information hidden there. He also wanted to ensure that the magic ring's powers were not ignored or taken for granted.

Everyone is busy searching for any signs that might lead to the success of their mission. Soon, they saw new letters forming on the wall as if written by an invisible hand. The big letters appeared and then slowly faded away as more letters were written. the time is now. you must act as one team. your next clues are in section four of the library. The group rushed to the fourth aisle, where they saw the enormous rat, as well as a mouse and a white cat. At the sight of the group, the animals scurried away, but everyone had seen them. By now the men had begun to put the puzzle together. Maybe, they thought, these animals were not what they appeared to be, just like the bird.

Things are starting to make sense now. Whatever the animals turned out to be, they hold the answers to their questions.

Paul led the group and was the first to step into the aisle. Everyone remembered that Paul was the only one allowed to touch things. As they moved on, however, one of the policemen became impatient and ignored the blackbird's directives, grabbing an old book from a shelf. Instantly his hand was glued to book, separating itself from the rest of his arm. The officer screamed. "I am in trouble!" he yelled. "Help! Please, anyone, help! Paul, please help me!"

Just as Paul arrived to see the gruesome sight, the blackbird made an appearance, saying, "I told you not to touch anything!" "I am sorry,

I didn't mean to," the officer said, writhing in pain. "I stumbled on the uneven floor, and when I tried to stop myself from falling, I accidentally touched the book."

"Fair enough," the blackbird said. "I must warn you one more time; pay attention where you walk." The blackbird then turned to Paul. "With your right hand, touch the officer's arm," the blackbird said. "With your left, touch the book. Then take the officer's arm and guide it to the book." Paul did exactly what the blackbird told him, and like magic, the officer was completely healed.

"The next man to have an accident like this will not be so fortunate," the blackbird added. "Go and continue your search. You have a lot to accomplish yet."

During all the commotion, the curious little mouse had emerged from underneath the shelves, looking for a hiding place from which it could watch what is happening. The mouse was able to watch people undetected, its ground-level view made it hard to see through the crowd. Soon enough, after it is over, the little mouse scampered back under the shelves as the men resumed snooping among the books. Evidently, the books had been sitting on the shelves for a long time because they were covered with dust and spider webs, and the shelves themselves were littered with dry, dead flies.

Being more cautious this time, the men paid close attention to every little movement around them; they were dead silent. Looking for anything, listening to any sound that might lead them in the right direction. Finally, while he was looking among the shelves, Paul's magic ring gave him a signal; a beam of light like a laser that connected to a gleaming book. Everyone stepped out of Paul's way as he moved toward the book. Finally, the moment that they had all been hoping and working for had arrived. All eyes followed the brilliant beam of light connecting the book to the magic ring.

The blackbird appeared and said, "You now have in your possession an especially important book. For some of us here, this is the book of life. When Paul has this book in his hand, I shall disappear, but not for long."

"Don't leave us," one officer begged. "We're getting so close!" The blackbird replied, "in a short while, you will understand everything.

Paul, you may now take the book in your hand. Do not open it now—just hold it close. Everyone, follow me."

While the bird spoke, the mouse, rat, and the white cat were starting to move and hid near a desk at the center of the room. Finally, the time has come. Then the blackbird took flight, carefully guiding the men toward the desk. Paul moved with the closed book in his hand and laid it on the middle of the table.

"The moment of truth is at hand," the blackbird said to him. "Paul, you may open the book now. It has been sitting on a shelf for so long I don't remember for sure if what you need is in the book or in a manuscript hidden in the book." Paul carefully opened the book and found a manuscript inside it. The blackbird said, "Take the manuscript out and read it." Paul removed the manuscript and read:

> *In AD 44, I was a warlock, a good warlock that is, doing good deeds for everyone. One day a bad warlock came to challenge me I did not know where he was from or who he was and what the real intention was. We fought. He was so powerful. I scampered away like a frightened rat and I found this cave. I was able and provide for my existence by befriending the people in the nearby village.*
>
> *Everything was running smoothly and peacefully until the bad warlock made an appearance again, this time disguised as a wolf. I did not know it was him, so I went about my daily business, never suspecting that the bad warlock was quietly following me.*
>
> *One day, I went to town and found a lovely mansion. There was a garage and an old barn on the property, and a gorgeous lake with a sandy beach that was perfect for long hours of relaxing and fishing. It was perfect for me. But I cannot take the risk and decided to stay in the cave where I feel safer. I went there occasionally to fish. I loved that place.*
>
> *Everything was running smoothly. The wolf disappeared, and for a couple of years I provided for myself and worked honestly blending with the villagers; I certainly did not steal from or hurt anyone. Everybody in the town was friendly. The people worked together graciously, helping each other as they went about their daily lives.*
>
> *I even started to decorate the cave—as you may notice, I bought and installed candles. Since I am an architect, I built several floors of living space connected by ladders. It took me a long time to make this moldy cave pleasant.*

> *I was on my way to the village one day when a wolf entered the cave. Oddly, it stayed there motionless, looked me in the eye and I can see it was beaming with hatred. It changed its appearance and become the bad warlock I was trying hard to avoid.*
>
> *He cast a spell on me, and I began to age rapidly until I became an incredibly old man who could barely move at all.*
>
> *Then he said, "I will restore your youth but all of your friends in the village will hate you. Until the day comes—if it ever does—that someone would discover this manuscript, learned of your true story and free you. You dirty scoundrel will suffer. I will make it impossible to find however for the meantime you will remain my possession. The people in the town will cast you out and never be welcomed there again The beautiful lake you love, the lake by which you feed yourself, you will never see it again. You will be doomed in this cave."*

As Paul concluded the first part of the manuscript, the manuscript began shining so brightly that Paul appeared as a gleaming silhouette. Everyone in the library trembled at the sight.

"This is more than I can take," said one officer. "Never in my entire life did I think I would ever see anything like this." His words broke the silence. Paul froze, eagerly waiting what would happen next. The blackbird reappeared.

The blackbird told Harry to step forward and stand at Paul's right side. Everyone cleared the way for Harry, who appeared anxious. Clearly, he preferred that someone else is assigned the task, but he approached and stood at Paul's right side anyway. At that moment he became, like Paul, a silhouette of light. Then the blackbird said, "Harry, put your right hand on Paul's right shoulder." Harry did so, and the manuscript returned to normal, with a new page appearing. The group members noticed the bird's disappearance and wondered aloud where it might have gone. Then Paul continued to read the manuscript:

> *A century-old secret lies within the walls and rooms of this cave and the clues to remove the spell. Once the spell was removed, no one will be able to enter this cave again. On the lowest level of this cave, where the good warlock once made his residence, you will find a crystal ball. Chosen one, you must be the only one to touch it, just as you are the only one who may hold this manuscript. If someone touches it other than you, the curse will*

go on forever. Nothing and no one will be able to cast it out. Go on, a family is waiting to be saved.

As he read, Paul felt his hand weaken. He wanted to drop the manuscript.

If you drop the manuscript, then I will live forever and you all will be my possession.

Poor Harry was trembling; he was beginning to regret having volunteered for this mission. He saw a whole lifetime of memories flashing in front of him; he could still see himself exactly where he was when his whole family disappeared. As memories flooded Harry's mind, Paul continued to read the manuscript:

As for the helper of the chosen one, you are the only one who may wave the magic wand: you have been given this role as a reward for your dedication. It is important for you to know that all the animals in the cave are human. Now all of you must pay close attention: no one can leave this library without saving all of them.

At this point Paul paused, and every one of the group members seemed to exclaim all at once, "This is unbelievable! "One officer said, "At one point I suspected that was the case. Honestly, how could a bird talk or understand or even follow a conversation?"

"Yes, indeed," Harry said, "and the most peculiar way of finding the truth." Paul continued to read the last part of the manuscript:

You will find a blackbird, a mouse, a rat, a white cat, two huge ants, and a father and mother raccoon. These animals are hidden in this library. As for the raccoons, they can be found with the help of the rest of the family. Do not attempt to find the raccoons first; that would be extremely dangerous. You must find the animals in the order they are named in this manuscript, beginning with the blackbird; otherwise, the mission will take more time to complete. There is one more who disappeared after the family you are seeking here. That person suffered the same thing they did. He is not here, but one of the family members will know where he is and will come forward to solve the disappearance.

That was the end of the manuscript, and Paul placed it carefully back into the century-old book. He knew that those last part were intended for him and his family. He walked back to the fourth aisle to deposit the book back into its place among the other old books on the shelves.

Now the focus had shifted from finding the book that had given them the manuscript to find the magic wand. Paul knew his magic ring could give him the advantage of finding it more quickly, but he also remembered what the manuscript had said; they should work as a team. So, everyone is on the lookout to find the magic wand. The investigators were trying to find codes and numbers without touching or moving anything. And everyone is watching Harry, who is anxious and more fragile than they thought.

With the focus now on Harry, Paul can contrite more. Paul just wanted to get this whole nightmare over and done with. Working as a team, just like the manuscript stated, the men combed the library again. That is when Paul found a little secret door in the library wall. He examined it, but it is locked. Then he remembered what the blackbird had said, anything Paul wanted would be granted to him once he wore the magic ring. Paul did not know if this is still true, but he took the chance to ask. Looking at the magic ring, he said, "Magic ring, help me find the key to this little door."

Suddenly, as if he were being pushed by a mysterious force, he was guided to the other end of the library, the first thing that he saw is a little key hooked on the wall, shining brightly as if saying, "I am here—come and get me!" Paul grabbed the little key and then joined the others to show them what he had found. Together they walked to the little door and watched Paul try the key in the lock. Sure enough, it fit. Paul turned the key, unlocked the little door, and opened it—and there was the magic wand.

"Okay now," Harry said. "I am a bit nervous, but I can do this." Everyone stayed out the way of Harry, who picked up the magic wand and had control of its movement. His first task is the blackbird; he had to touch it with the wand to turn it back into the person it had been.

Paul said, "Here is the list showing the order we have to follow to solve the problem. First, we must touch the blackbird. Second the mouse. The third will be the rat. Fourth is a white cat, followed by numbers five and six—two ants. Then, of course, there are the raccoons, which I assume are the parents."

All Harry had to do is point the wand toward it and say, "I Harry order you to come back to your real identity." And so, the men's game of hide-and-seek with the blackbird began. Some of the officers stepped just outside the library doors to see if the blackbird is outside the room and they saw it fly in, they would close the doors behind it.

The search went on for about half an hour until one of the investigators shouted, "Over here, Harry! Hurry! It looks like the blackbird is dying!" Harry and Paul both knew that the blackbird is playing a little game, just as it had the other times. Nevertheless, Harry stepped quickly toward the blackbird, pointed the magic wand at it and said,

"I, Harry, order you to come back to your real identity." The blackbird disappeared, and there is a young woman standing in its place. The men could not believe their eyes.

"How long you have been a bird?" asked the investigator. "For at least two years," the young woman replied.

"So, your family vanished just two years ago? But according to the manuscript, the bad warlock was not heard of a century ago. How can that be?"

"Well," she said, "we just bought the mansion when my family and I discovered this cave. We explored it and, on our way, out we changed. That is how we turned into the animals you began seeing the first day you bought the house. It is our home, was our home.

"From time to time, two of our family—a rat and a mouse—would return to the mansion to see what is happening there. That is how the rat met a woman there in the kitchen. She was terrified." "That's my wife, Eva" replied Paul. "And that rat also terrified my daughters that same night."

"I am so sorry the rat scared your daughters—they were probably in the rat's bed," the young lady said. "Now we have to find the rest of my family. Most of them are here in the library. This is where we all hide out when we sense danger." "Yes," Paul said. "According to the manuscript, we have to proceed in a certain order. Next, we must find the mouse. We certainly can use all the help we can get."

The young lady smiled and said, "By the way, my name is Claire, and I will help find the rest of my family. Let me call the mouse." Claire made a loud, clear, high-pitched sound, waited for a few moments, and then repeated it, but there is no response. She looked worried. "Maybe someone stepped on it," she said. "It's not responding. You may want to go back to the aisle where you found me."

Paul rushed back to the aisle, give the area a second look, and, sure enough, something terrible had happened: someone had stepped on the poor, small mouse. Luckily, it is still alive but barely. The rest of the group gathered around, nervously remembering the strict order not to step on any of the animals. The men panicked and thought the small mouse was dead. But Harry pointed the magic wand toward the mouse and said, "I, Harry, order you to come back to your real identity."

The mouse, just like the blackbird, evaporated, and a young boy appeared before them. "Hello," he said cheerfully. "My name is Anthony. That is my sister, Claire. I cannot believe I am finally free! Thank you." The siblings hugged each other for a long time. Then, with tears rolling down his face, Anthony asked, "Where are our brothers and sisters?"

"Somewhere in the library," Claire answered. "Why don't you try to call the rat? You two were always awfully close." "Sure," Anthony said. "Let me try." Anthony made a distinctive call and then waited for an answer, but there was no response. Surprised, Anthony said, "That's the first time that the rat hasn't answered my call. I wonder if it is all right. Maybe it's just too scared to come out." Anthony tried one more time, again without success. He then turned to his sister. "Claire, I think it's scared."

"Maybe so," she said, nodding. "Try to explain to the rat that there's no need to be afraid. It's okay to come out now." So, Anthony tried to call the rat again. He still did not see the rat; he had a clue where it might be. He turned to Paul and asked, "Would it be possible for me to rescue the rat by myself?

Paul shook his head. "According to the manuscript, we all have to work as a team—that means not too far away from each another—for the mission to succeed." "Well, I know the rat is very afraid of strangers because so many people have tried to kill it," Anthony said.

"That makes sense," Harry said. He looked over at Paul. "Since I have the magic wand and you have the magic ring, I am sure we can work something out here. If all of you stand about five feet away from us, then I am sure the rat will feel more secure." They all agreed and let Harry and Anthony walk toward the area where the rat is likely hiding. Anthony made the noise again, and this time, sure enough, the rat reluctantly emerged. Harry pointed the magic wand at the rat immediately before it would go into hiding again and said, "I, Harry, order you to come back to your real identity."

The rat is gone, and another girl appeared. "Anthony!" she said, smiling, and the two hugged each other, crying. "It is so nice to see you again. It has sure been a long time." The girl looked over at Harry. "Who are you?" she asked. "I am Harry. And what's your name?"

"My name is Catherine. Thank you so much for putting an end to my misery—and theirs," she said, walking from Anthony to Claire and giving her a big hug. "Where are the others?" she asked excitedly. "Are they safe? Have they already been rescued?"

"No," answered Claire. "Maybe you should try to call the white cat." "Yes, certainly," Catherine said. Catherine made a loud meow and waited for a few seconds, but nothing happened. "I'll bet the cat is out there sleeping as usual. I will have to go find it," she said.

Catherine stepped out of the library and again made a loud meow. Meanwhile, the policemen and investigators were questioning the rescued siblings, asking them how this whole thing had started. The siblings were so overwhelmed; they cannot believe that a happy reunion is happening now. Finally, the realization seemed to hit them that the rescue is truly taking place.

Catherine came back inside the library and immediately saw the white cat sleeping. She began talking to it in a soft, low voice, as Harry pointed the magic wand again and said, "I, Harry, order you to come back to your real identity."

Another boy is standing in front of them. The investigators asked, "What's your name?" "My name is Randy," the boy answered shyly. The investigators checked the list and saw that the only animals left in the library were the two ants. Encouraged by their success, they asked Randy if he knew where the ants might be. Randy, who is happily chatting with his brother and sisters, replied, "All I know is that the ants were kept in a locked place. Because they ate wood, they were locked up." "Where?" asked Paul.

"I don't know," he said. "All I can tell you is that they are in the middle of the wall." This is another head-scratcher. How could they figure out exactly where this place might be?

Then Paul thought of the ring. "Magic ring," he said, "where is this secret place in the wall?" Immediately the ring emitted a ray of light toward a little door in the wall, something they had not notice before. Harry, followed by the whole group, walked toward it. To his surprise, he found that the door is just a flat piece of rock, with no keyhole. "How do we get this to open?" he asked Randy. "One of the ants has a number on it," the boy replied.

Paul felt himself flush; he had written down the number but left it at home. How could he be so careless to leave it? He said, "I know where the number is—at my house. I just forgot to bring it with me. I do have the one that was on the leg of the blackbird."

Catherine exclaimed, "You have that number with you? Let me see it." Paul nervously took the number out of his pocket and showed it to her. "Yes, I recognize this number!" she said. "It's a good thing you brought it with you. We will need that later. Keep it safe." Then Catherine walked over to the wall and looked at the door but saw nothing. Randy walked up behind her. "We must open that door," he said. "I don't want to leave without them."

"Wait!" said Paul. "I have an idea." He approached the little door and asked Harry to point the wand at it; Harry touched it with the end of the magic wand and asked it to reveal the secret code. Sure enough, some numbers appeared right next to the door:

25901706

The little door popped open, revealing two frightened ants huddled together. Harry took the magic wand and said, "I, Harry, order you to come back to your real identity." In an instant, a young boy and girl appeared. "Well, how are you guys doing?" Harry said softly. "It must have been hard for you to be locked up like this all the time." "Yes," the boy said. "And I hate chewing on woods. It sucks." One of the investigators asked, "What are your names?" "My name is Luke." "I am Gloria."

With that, the boy and girl ran to see their big sisters and brothers. Everyone is in tears. "I missed you so badly every day," Luke said. "I knew you had the chance to go out while we were kept in that little room." It is a happy reunion, and spirits were all high. Tears of joy and loving hugs are excessive that it melted the men's heart.

During happiness, however, a problem occurred: the children were thrilled to be together again but started to worry because they did not know where their parents are kept. All they knew is that in the big room there were two raccoons, but they never suspected that these were, in fact, their father and mother. They remembered that when they had been cursed, their parents had already disappeared.

Sensing their concern, Harry said, "We will find them. We also had to help the raccoons okay?" The children began wandering around the library, looking for clues to where their parents might be. Somehow the children seemed to know that this is the last time they would step into the library. The cave became their second home. Yes, a home full of bad memories.

The thought of leaving now is breaking their hearts because they feared that when they left, they would be leaving their parents behind, and any hope of finding them would vanish forever. The children were free, and everyone wanted to make sure that no clue had been overseen. Paul carefully scoured every inch of the library, asking the magic ring if there is anything that they had overlooked there. The ring did not answer, so Paul decided to call off the search in the library. Now it is time to search the bottom of the cave—but how could they reach it now that the blackbird had changed back into its human form?

Paul asked Claire if she knew how the ladders operated. "Any idea?" he said, "when you were the blackbird, you're the one who made things move around here."

"Yes, I do," she replied. "Let me show you." She then went to the wall opposite the ladders and located a hidden switch. She flipped the switch, and one ladder began moving—the same ladder that had transferred the group one at a time to the library. Now, however, the situation is different because the mean blackbird is now a nice young woman making their task as effortless as possible. The spell that had been cast on the ladder is lifted. Going down the bottom of the cave is a piece of cake. Harry is delighted and more relaxed now. The children's mood in the room was contagious.

The men are exhausted and hungry but hopeful, everyone knew that their mission in the cave is about to come to an end. As they moved down to the basement, they decided to look at the other floors in case there were instructions of some sort. Mistake is not an option for them right at that moment. They had explored one floor after the other, they had a chance to see the comfortable lifestyle the good warlock had created for himself. When the group was on the second floor, the magic ring emitted a laser-like beam of light. Harry followed by Claire and some other members of the group followed it.

The rest of the party moved on to the first floor. Those who had been part of a rescue team recognized it as the place where they had to wait for hours until the blackbird allowed them to enter the cave.

Harry and the others still on the second floor, they have not found the parents yet. Paul wondered when the search would cease. He wanted to go home, take a bath and rest. Claire vaguely remembered that some strange activity had occurred there but did not know what it is. Now she is dying to find out what had happened there.

Claire explained to the investigators that when the curse was cast on them. She had been told that the day would come that the curse will be lifted if everyone followed the bad warlock's orders. She is grateful to the team for rescuing her and her siblings, but now she is more focused on finding her parents. She had the feeling that they were in the cave or not too far from it.

Claire, Harry, and the group arrived at the place where the light is shining. They looked around and at first did not see anything special. Claire had a vague knowledge of the room making the search rather difficult. She noticed a small flash of light. She called out to the group, "It looks like something is there." Harry pointed out his magic wand. "Reveal to me what you are," he said. A new set of numbers started to appear on the rock:

$$5\ 6\ 8\ 4\ 1\ 0\ 0$$

Another code means another door, Paul thought. One member of the group wrote the numbers down, and then they went on, leaving the second floor. But then the ladder stopped working. Luckily enough, Claire knew where to go to restart it. She turned it back on and rejoined the group, who had been waiting for her to get it operating again. Soon everyone is together at the lowest level, where they hoped to find the raccoons. Claire ran over to her brothers and sisters, telling them to stick together and be cautious. None of the children have the faintest idea they were an inch away from rescuing their parents.

Harry led the children and men through the first level. They could tell that the good warlock had been rich and powerful; there were stacks of gold lying around, and most of the men found it very tempting to pick up a few gold coins and hide them in their pockets. However, they remembered the investigator who had lost his hand when it got stuck to the book that he had touched, and that stopped them from picking up any gold. The blackbird is gone now, but they had not forgotten, it had warned them that the next one to disobey would not be so lucky and might even perish. Cursed gold, they thought just to fight the urge of picking it up.

They arrived at an extremely large door, probably the entryway to the good warlock's room. It could only be opened with a code, and they already have it. Claire punched in the code and the door opened to reveal an exceptionally clean room illuminated by candlelight. Really? the group thought these raccoons were clean animals if this is their room. The cleanliness of the room is a good indication that whoever or whatever is living there had some sanitation skills.

Harry is the first one to step in, followed by the children and then the rest of the group. Armed with the magic wand, Harry soon is in full control of the situation now. He is adamant to make use of the temporary power he had in his hands.

The children recognized the area because more than once they had been told to stay there. They remembered playing hide-and-seek as animals.

Before long Claire spotted the first raccoon, which did not seem so happy being disturbed by strangers. Harry took his wand and said, "I, Harry, order you to come back to your real identity."

A man appeared, and all the children ran into his arms, which he opened wide to receive them. "Oh, you must be the father?" one of the policemen asked. "My name is Henry," the man said.

"You must be the Henry I have spent two years looking for!" the policeman exclaimed. "There have been all sorts of rumors around town saying someone had done something bad to you and your family, but none of the theories made sense, and none of my interrogations gave me any clues that could help move the investigation forward."

Henry turned to Harry. "Listen," he said, "I know where my wife is kept. Let me guide you to her. Please save her." Without wasting a moment, Henry led Harry to the hiding place of Lucia, his wife who also had been transformed into a raccoon. Pointing the magic wand, Harry said for the last time, "I, Harry, order you to come back to your real identity."

Lucia appeared, ecstatic to be reunited with her husband and children. The children were exuberant and rushed into their mother's arms, crying. "No wonder we always felt welcome here," Claire said. "We always sensed that we belonged together."

"Okay, that's about it! We are all tired and hungry. I see it's finally time to go home now.", one of the investigators said.

With the whole family reunited, the men were well on its way out of the cave. Paul forgot that he is still wearing the magic ring while walking out he suddenly turned into a statue. Nothing is to be carried out of the cave, the group soon realized that the ring might be the problem. One group member suggested that Harry might be able to restore Paul using the magic wand. Harry went back to the place where he threw the magic wand and retrieved it. "Let me try," Harry said, and with the end of the wand, he touched Paul, who immediately returned to normal. Paul took the magic ring from his finger and threw it far into the cave. Then he walked out of the cave unscathed.

Harry had wisely hurled the magic wand the very moment that Paul came back to normal. He, too, walked out of the cave safely. The rest of the men followed, and soon the entire group is heading back to the mansion. As they were walking, they heard a loud boom coming from the direction of the cave when they turned around, they saw only smoke coming out of the top of the mountains. The cave collapsed burying the warlock's secret within. They turned again and continued walking, having just one desire at this moment; to go home. The family of Henry and Lucia, finally free and on their way back to the town, thanked their rescuers over and over for all their effort and courage.

They reached a hill and farther below saw the mansion that had once belonged to them. Henry said quietly, "I know that we are not the only people to have suffered because of this mansion." When Paul heard that, he said, "Yeah. It's hard and painful." Claire turned to him. "I owe you one," she said. "I will repay you for what you did for me and my family."

"I missed my son so much," Paul said with a heavy heart. "When you were a blackbird you pooped at me and my son. I will never forget that."

"I am so sorry I did explain myself back in the cave," Claire said. "That was supposed to be a warning, come on—I didn't do that on purpose." "No worries at all," Paul said smiling, feeling triumphant with his teasing.

"I have an idea about what happened," Claire said. "I'll talk to you about it another time. For now, we need to find a place to stay. Do not tell me to stay in your place because we are not going back to that mansion. No way!" At this point, Harry joined the conversation and asked Claire if she recognized him.

"Yes, I do," she said, "I recognized you and remembered of all of the bad things you said about me as a blackbird." She smiled. "How many people did you save from that mansion?" "Not many, the house was back on the market exactly five months after your family vanished." "And you, Paul—are you the owner now?" Claire asked.

"Yes, I am, unfortunately. I brought my family here because I fell in love with the place when I saw it. Since then, we have been stuck in misery. I lost one of my sons." Paul took a deep breath and added, "I know I will find my son. If we were able to rescue your family, well, my son is next on the list. I already know I can count on you to help."

"Of course," Claire said. "Paul, I can only imagine what you are going through right now. Do not give up; stick with it, because I know that you will find your son, alive and well. There is so much that we need to talk about Paul." "I know," replied Paul. "Let's get together as soon as possible." "You have it," she said.

Paul's children were at the lake when they heard the big boom and saw smoke coming out of the mountain. Not long afterward, they saw a group of people walking down the road with their father in the lead. Behind him were policemen and other rescue members, as well as new faces: six children and two adults. Paul's children could not believe what they were seeing. They all ran toward their father and gave him a big hug. Proud of their father finally finding the lost family. But the one question still lies unanswered, where is Angelo?

www.ingramcontent.com/pod-product-compliance
Lightning Source LLC
LaVergne TN
LVHW091535070526
838199LV00001B/72